YOUR INNER HEDGEHOG

Alexander McCall Smith

ABACUS

First published in Great Britain in 2021 by Little, Brown
This paperback edition published in 2022 by Abacus

1 3 5 7 9 10 8 6 4 2

Copyright © Alexander McCall Smith 2021
Illustrations copyright © Iain McIntosh, 2020

The moral right of the author has been asserted.

All characters and events in this publication, other than those
clearly in the public domain, are fictitious and any resemblance
to real persons, living or dead, is purely coincidental.

All rights reserved.
No part of this publication may be reproduced, stored in a
retrieval system, or transmitted, in any form or by any means, without
the prior permission in writing of the publisher, nor be otherwise circulated
in any form of binding or cover other than that in which it is published
and without a similar condition including this condition being
imposed on the subsequent purchaser.

A CIP catalogue record for this book is available from the British Library.

ISBN 978-0-349-14451-1

Typeset in Galliard by M Rules
Printed and bound in Great Britain by Clays Ltd, Elcograf S.p.A

Papers used by Abacus are from well-managed forests
and other responsible sources.

Abacus
An imprint of
Little, Brown Book Group
Carmelite House
50 Victoria Embankment
London EC4Y 0DZ

An Hachette UK Company
www.hachette.co.uk

www.littlebrown.co.uk

3/22

0 1 SEP 2022
1 1 AUG 2023

14 APR 2022
0 7 JUL 2022
0 7 JUL 2022

0 AUG 2022

1 1 AUG 2022
2 8 SEP 2022

WITHDRAWN

Books should be returned or renewed by the last
date above. Renew by phone **03000 41 31 31** or
online *www.kent.gov.uk/libs*

Libraries Registration & Archives   CUSTOMER SERVICE EXCELLENCE   Kent County Council kent.gov.uk

devouring' Marcel Berlins, *Guardian*

'When it comes to the light touch, no one beats Alexander
McCall Smith' James Naughtie, *Financial Times*

By Alexander McCall Smith

This book is for Duncan and Hilary Menzies

eins

VON IGELFELD

Clouds upon the Horizon

Professor Dr Dr (*honoris causa*) (*mult.*) Moritz-Maria von Igelfeld came from a distinguished family about whom little is known, other than they had existed, as von Igelfelds, for a very long time. The obscurity of their early history in no way detracted from the family's distinction; in fact, if anything, it added to it. Anybody can find their way into the history books by doing something egregiously unpleasant: starting a local war, stealing the land and property of others, being particularly vindictive towards neighbours: all of these are well-understood routes to fame and can lead to immense distinction, titles and honorifics. Most people who today are dukes or earls are there because of descent from markedly successful psychopaths. Their ancestors were simply higher achievers than other people's when it came to deceit, expropriation, selfishness and murder. That none of these attributes tends to be recorded in family coats of arms is testimony to the ability of people to brush over or even completely ignore the saliences of the inconvenient past. Coats of arms of armigerous families therefore tend to embody devices that bear no relation to the means by which those families' prominence was achieved. There are no bloody knives in heraldry, no hidden trapdoors, no evicted widows, impoverished orphans or betrayed allies. There are, by contrast, plenty of suns, moons, ears of corn and ships. If weapons are depicted, these are stylised and, most importantly, innocently sheathed.

The von Igelfeld coat of arms was somewhat unusual, relating directly to the family name, in its English translation meaning *hedgehog-field*. The hedgehog is not a common heraldic device; indeed, it is thought to occur in no other coat of arms, German or otherwise. It is not generally considered a noble creature. Lions and unicorns abound in heraldry because they evoke, respectively, courage and charm; the modest hedgehog, by contrast, bears few associations. It scurries about the undergrowth on business of its own devising. It threatens nobody other than small grubs and insects, for whom there is anyway generally little sympathy. The hedgehog is the hero of no legend, no myth, apart from the Grimms' *Der Hase und der Igel*. There is no patron saint to protect it, no Greek hero to represent it, no Hindu god whose transformational form was the hedgehog. Why the von Igelfeld family should have adopted the hedgehog, both as their name and their symbol, is uncertain. Family tradition has it that they once lived in close proximity to a field renowned for its hedgehogs, but where this field was, and even if it ever existed, is far from clear. Another tradition has it that a von Igelfeld ancestor was once saved by a hedgehog, although how a hedgehog might be capable of saving anybody has never been revealed. Dogs have saved the lives of humans, as have horses, and even, famously, Capitoline geese, but never have hedgehogs been credited with such service to humanity.

The family came originally from the eastern reaches of Bavaria. The earliest von Igelfeld is recorded in the sixteenth century, in a reference in a land charter granted to a Heinrich von Igelfeld, proprietor of a farm endowed with two active mills. After that, there are one hundred and twenty years of obscurity until another document records the transfer of a substantial estate to one Franz-Josef, Graf von Igelfeld, now apparently a count. Some eighty years later, the title seems to have disappeared, and the next von Igelfeld to be mentioned in any records has been demoted from *Graf* to *Freiherr*. That particular von Igelfeld owned a substantial parcel of land and may be assumed to have been wealthy, but a brief letter that has survived in the family archives refers to the problems that resulted from his having forgotten where his land was. And that difficulty dictated the fate of the family over the following years: there was an estate – somewhere – but nobody knew where it was.

By the time of Moritz-Maria's father, Hans-Christian von Igelfeld, the family had largely lost contact with the land, although at least one uncle continued to be landed.

Although the name was suggestive of nobility, the family was now firmly rooted in the professional classes in and around Munich. Hans-Christian had been a professor of surgery who wrote a widely used book on the correction of incorrectly set fractures; his brother, Casper, was an engineer who specialised in designing Archimedes' screws. The family had lived in modest comfort and would have disappeared into the *haute bourgeoisie* were it not for the unusual name and for their continuing sense that they belonged elsewhere, in rather grander circumstances than those in which they currently found themselves.

After completing his school education at a classical gymnasium, Moritz-Maria had enrolled at the University of Heidelberg. It was there that he had first met Florianus Prinzel, the son of a banker, a member of a student *Korps*, and highly popular for his sporting prowess. The relationship between the two young men was very much that of one between scholar-poet and hero-athlete. Von Igelfeld admired Prinzel for his social ease and his bravery, but realised that he could never match his social and sporting achievements. At that stage, of course, he had had no idea that years later they would find themselves as close colleagues in the Institute of Romance Philology at the University of Regensburg. Nor would he have imagined that the friendship between them would be very much resented by another colleague, Professor Dr Detlev Amadeus Unterholzer, who came from an obscure potato-growing family, and who had long been envious of von Igelfeld's noble background. Of course, Unterholzer had other reasons to bear a grudge against von Igelfeld; these centred on von Igelfeld's role in the events that had led to the amputation of three of Unterholzer's dachshund's four legs, requiring the dog thereafter to get around on a set of wheels strapped to his abdomen. That incident was still occasionally referred to by Unterholzer, in an unmistakably resentful tone, prompting von Igelfeld to change the subject as quickly as possible whenever any mention was made of dachshunds.

After Heidelberg, von Igelfeld had undertaken doctoral studies at the University of Regensburg. The subject of his doctoral thesis was linguistic shifts in the Portuguese language, with special reference to their occurrence in Brazil and Goa. This was to be the foundation, many years later, of his classic work *Portuguese Irregular Verbs*, a book of twelve hundred pages, hailed by many in the field as being the most significant single contribution to Romance linguistics in over a century. It was on the strength of that great work that von Igelfeld had received his call to a Chair in Regensburg. There he found himself working in the Institute of Romance Philology alongside Prinzel, who had returned from further studies in Paris, and Unterholzer, who had recently completed his *Habilitationsschrift* in Berlin. Von Igelfeld had heard from his contacts at the *Freie Universität* there that Unterholzer's work was 'not really first-rate' and that most of it was 'barely publishable'. This was tittle-tattle of the sort that abounds in academia, but von Igelfeld had noted it carefully and was once heard referring to 'our dear, weaker colleague, Herr Unterholzer'. That condescending description had been made in private, but its effect had lingered, and Unterholzer's work was thereafter rarely considered to be in the same league as that of von Igelfeld or Prinzel. Academia is full of injustices, and this was certainly one of them.

There were only three professors in the Institute of Romance Philology, although there were eleven untenured researchers, nine of them allocated to the three full professors, each of whom had three. The remaining two, both named Müller, were independent, having completed the necessary qualifications needed to take up a Chair if one were to become vacant. These two both eyed the Chairs occupied by von Igelfeld, Prinzel and Unterholzer with ill-concealed fascination, and secretly would have been delighted if illness or other disaster were to strike one, or preferably two, members of the professoriate. Occasionally this led to muttered remarks passing between the two of them, such as: 'Did you think Professor von Igelfeld looked slightly pale this morning, Herr Müller? I do hope he's not sickening for anything serious – or even fatal.' And that might bring forth the response, 'You're right, Herr Müller. He would be sorely missed were he to succumb to some dreadful illness – which heaven forfend, of course.' And then each would silently reflect on just what would happen were von Igelfeld's Chair to be vacated. Prinzel and Unterholzer would both apply for it, they imagined, and this would mean that the resulting vacancy further down the academic food chain would become available to one of them. Each Müller, of course, thought of himself as being markedly superior to the other, but both knew that the resulting competition would not be a pretty one. 'They'd sell their own grandmother for a Chair' is a common criticism of those on the lower rungs of the academic ladder, which raises questions as to just why so few German professors appear to have extant grandmothers. That is a complex issue, though, and one for another time.

The other senior member of the Institute's staff was the Librarian, Herr Huber. Although not a professor, Herr Huber was allowed to use the Senior Coffee Room along with von Igelfeld, Prinzel and Unterholzer; the Müllers were not afforded the same privilege, but were permitted to keep the milk for their coffee in the Senior Coffee Room fridge, as long as they did not attempt to make their coffee there. For that purpose they had a small kitchen at the end of a corridor, although this did not have anywhere to sit.

Herr Huber was in his early forties and was a graduate of the University of Munich. He also had a diploma in Advanced Cataloguing from the Library School of the University of Hamburg, and a further diploma in Linguistic Librarianship from the University of Amsterdam. Until recently he had been a bachelor, but was now married to a woman from Bonn. They lived just outside town in a very small house on the edge of a forest – 'Rather like Hansel and Gretel,' observed von

Igelfeld, much to the amusement of his colleagues.

Herr Huber had an aunt who was a permanent resident of a nursing home in Regensburg. He visited her every day, taking her pastries he bought for her from the *Konditorei* near the Institute. On these visits the aunt would regale her nephew with items of news from the nursing home, and these in due course would be passed on by Herr Huber during the Institute's morning coffee break.

'My aunt has a new pill,' he announced one morning. 'Until now she has been prescribed five pills a day: three to be taken in the morning, and two in the evening. Or is it the other way round? I think it may be two in the morning and three in the evening.'

'I think you told us last week,' said Professor Dr Unterholzer, with a deliberately heavy stress on *last week*, 'that it was two in the morning and four in the evening.'

Herr Huber, though, was adamant. 'No, she certainly does *not* have six pills a day. I know that, Herr Professor, because there is a man in a room near hers who indeed has six pills. He is a certain Herr Lucien Hoffmeyer, a tall man of cheerful disposition, who was the Secretary of a bank in Munich until his retirement. He told me himself that he takes six pills a day, and I don't think that is a detail that somebody who was the Secretary of a bank would get wrong.'

'These pills that your aunt takes,' asked Professor Dr Dr Prinzel. 'What are they for?'

'One is for blood pressure,' said Herr Huber. 'My aunt

does not have excessive blood pressure, which is what many people suffer from these days. Her blood pressure is too low, if anything. You need a certain amount of blood pressure to ensure that the blood reaches the head. If your blood pressure is too low, the blood itself does not circulate effectively. It stays in the lower regions of the body and does not reach the head in the quantities needed. That, I believe, is what her red pill does. Another pill is to ensure that she does not retain too much water in her system, and another one, I believe, deals with heart arrhythmia, from which she suffered even before her admission to the nursing home.'

'I see,' said von Igelfeld.

'Yes,' said Herr Huber. 'Mind you, sometimes there are other things to think about in the nursing home, apart from pills and such matters. Last week, for example, one of the fire sprinklers was triggered and soaked several chairs – quite badly, in fact. One of them was ruined, I believe. It was a false alarm, of course, but I take the view that it is far better for these things to be activated too often rather than not work at all when a real fire comes along.'

Herr Huber was assisted in his duties as Librarian by three colleagues: the newly appointed Dr Hilda Schreiber-Ziegler, a large and rather brassy woman who was his deputy; Herr Markus Herring, a man in his early thirties who was a keen marathon-runner; and Dr Jorge Martensen, who was Danish on his father's side and German on his mother's. Dr Martensen had a doctorate in semiotics, the science of signs and symbols, and was the author of a pamphlet on the sign language of Cistercian monks, of which the Library now possessed seven copies.

When first she had been appointed, Dr Schreiber-Ziegler had assumed that as Deputy Librarian she would be entitled to use the Institute's Senior Coffee Room. On her first day in the Institute she had followed Herr Huber into those precincts, only to be greeted with sudden and complete silence. Consumed with embarrassment, Herr Huber had rapidly engaged her in a long conversation about nursing homes, while his three colleagues buried their noses in the morning papers.

It was von Igelfeld who took it upon himself to take the Librarian aside and remind him of the rules of access that had always been applied to the Senior Coffee Room.

'There has never been any doubt,' he said, 'but that use of the Senior Coffee Room is reserved for the holders of full Chairs, Herr Huber, and, as a special concession, *full* librarians. You are a full librarian, and of course nobody would dispute *your* right to take coffee with us. But Dr Schreiber-Ziegler is, as you of all people must know, a *deputy* librarian, which is clearly *not* the same thing as a full librarian.'

Herr Huber protested that he had not invited his deputy to accompany him. 'She just got up and followed me into the Senior Coffee Room,' he said. 'As you know, Herr Professor, I am not a radical of any stripe. I would never challenge this sort of convention.'

'I very much appreciate that, Herr Huber,' said von

Igelfeld, with the air of a judge obliged to uphold an onerous law. 'It is certainly the case that you do not have a reputation for radicalism. And yet, you will appreciate why it is that we must hold you responsible for your deputy.'

Herr Huber looked miserable. 'I shall not find it easy to talk to her about this,' he said. 'It will be very hard to tell her that she cannot join us for coffee – especially when she said to me how much she enjoyed this morning's coffee break, even if nobody spoke to her.'

Von Igelfeld sympathised with Herr Huber's embarrassment, and it was for this reason that he had prepared in advance a compromise that he now revealed to the discomfited Librarian.

'In order to make it easier for you,' said von Igelfeld, 'I propose that we redefine the rules. Although Dr Schreiber-Ziegler will not be allowed to use the Coffee Room on normal mornings, I see no reason why she should not be allowed to use it *on those occasions when you are, for any reason, absent from the Institute*. We shall then deem her to be you – temporarily. This may not happen very frequently, but that is not the point. The point, you'll agree, is the principle involved.'

Dr Schreiber-Ziegler listened carefully when Herr Huber conveyed this ruling to her. When he had finished, she stared at him with a look of astonishment that slowly became a broad grin. 'Are you serious?' she asked.

Herr Huber squirmed with embarrassment. 'But of course I'm serious, Dr Schreiber-Ziegler. I wouldn't joke

13

about a matter of this nature.' He paused, and looked at her reproachfully. 'In fact, I wouldn't joke about anything.'

'I've never heard such absurd nonsense in my life,' Dr Schreiber-Ziegler blurted out. 'Hedgehog-Field, Prinzel and what's-his-name, the one who looks like a potato . . .'

'Professor Dr Unterholzer,' provided Herr Huber, and immediately blushed bright red. He would never describe a senior professor of the University as resembling a potato, and yet he had somehow been tricked into doing just that. This Dr Schreiber-Ziegler, he decided, was potentially a very dangerous woman indeed.

'Yes, him – well, all three of them,' continued Dr Schreiber-Ziegler. 'Who on earth do they think they are?'

Herr Huber was at a loss. This was as seditious a conversation as he had ever been involved in, and it filled him with foreboding. If deputy librarians could speak with such contempt for full professors, what might they say, in private, about full librarians?

'I think we should be very careful in what we say,' he cautioned. 'An ill-judged word could cause immense damage if it were to get back to those for whose ears it was not intended.'

Dr Schreiber-Ziegler gave him a challenging stare. '*Phooey*,' she said after a while. 'That's what I think of them and their ridiculous rules. *Phooey*.' She paused. 'And you can tell them, Herr Huber. Tell them I say *phooey*.'

Herr Huber's shock now knew no limits. 'I certainly shall not,' he said.

He returned to his desk, uncertain how to proceed. He had been at the Institute for eighteen years now, and not once in that time had he encountered any expression of overt disrespect towards the authority of senior scholars. This, he thought, must have been what it was like to live in revolutionary France, just at the moment that the first whispered threats to Louis XVI were being heard in the streets – and look what had happened there: between the first stirrings of discontent and a full-blown uprising was but a short step. For a few moments he imagined Dr Schreiber-Ziegler as a *tricoteuse*, sitting beneath the guillotine, her knitting needles clicking busily as the tumbril delivered von Igelfeld, Prinzel and Unterholzer to their appointment with revolutionary justice. But wait – there was a fourth figure in the tumbril – and, in a moment of horror, Herr Huber saw that it was himself.

zwei

Dr Schreiber-Ziegler
Shows her Hand

O ver the following two weeks, nothing was said about the unfortunate incident in the Senior Coffee Room. If any credit was due for defusing the situation, that should undoubtedly have gone to Dr Schreiber-Ziegler, who started to bring with her a small vacuum flask labelled *Coffee* from which she poured herself a half-cup in the morning and a half-cup in the afternoon. This she drank – perhaps rather pointedly – while seated at her desk, in full view of Herr Huber and the other members of the Library staff. For a couple of days Herr Huber went off for his morning coffee by a circuitous route, avoiding walking directly past his deputy, but in due course he abandoned this and brazenly followed his normal route to the Senior Coffee Room.

Dr Schreiber-Ziegler had come to the Institute with glowing references, and it had not been long before the extraordinary efficiency and problem-solving ability referred to in those letters of recommendation had become evident.

Within a matter of days she had proposed, and begun to implement, improved cross-referencing in the Library's catalogues, and, not long after this, she had succeeded in negotiating a considerable discount for several journal subscriptions the Institute was considering cancelling on the grounds of cost. This last achievement, reported to von Igelfeld and Prinzel by Herr Huber, had attracted particularly warm praise from the two philologists.

'She may be of a radical temperament,' von Igelfeld had said, 'but she certainly seems to be able to save money.'

'It might be premature to suggest this,' Prinzel had ventured, 'but I can see her as a full librarian somewhere – one of these days. Who knows?'

'Who indeed?' echoed von Igelfeld.

It was Herr Herring who suggested to Herr Huber that a review should be carried out of the Library's policy on duplicates. 'We receive new books every day,' he said, 'and yet we are creating no new shelves. Sooner or later, we shall burst at the seams.'

Herr Huber agreed. 'This is a problem that every library faces,' he said. 'But where does one start?'

'The only solution, it seems to me,' said Herr Herring, 'is to remove unnecessary material. It's always hard to select what is going to go, but sometimes one simply has to grasp that particular nettle. We must remove duplicates.'

Herr Huber answered without hesitation. 'Yes, you are correct, Herr Herring. That, of course, requires an experienced eye – and I believe we have just the person for the job.'

He spoke that same day to Dr Schreiber-Ziegler, who had just finished a survey of the Library's holdings in French orthography and was looking for a new challenge.

'I shall start work immediately,' she said.

'And remember, Dr Schreiber-Ziegler,' said the Librarian, 'be ruthless. A policy of pruning should never be half-hearted.'

'You can leave it to me, Herr Huber,' said Dr Schreiber-Ziegler. 'I shall set myself a target of twenty metres of cleared shelf space, and I shall endeavour to meet it.'

'Pay particular attention to the French dictionaries,' said Herr Huber. 'I noticed the other day that we had four copies of Jean-François Féraud's *Dictionnaire critique de la langue française*. They are substantial volumes, and I would have thought that a single copy would be perfectly adequate.'

'I could not agree more,' said Dr Schreiber-Ziegler. 'I, too, had noticed an over-provision in that department. There are three copies, I believe, of the 1694 *Dictionnaire de l'Académie française*. Once again, a single copy would be all any library needs.'

Armed with Herr Huber's instructions – and authority – Dr Schreiber-Ziegler began her survey of duplicate copies, and very soon had identified over one hundred and thirty duplicates. These she began to remove from the shelves and place in boxes in a store-room, pending their valuation by the Rare Books Department of the University Library. Some of them, she believed, were of considerable value, and their sale would help to defray the growing costs of journal subscriptions.

At the end of that first week, Herr Huber received a visit from Dr Martensen, who knocked on his office door in his typically diffident way.

'I wonder if I could have a word with you on a rather delicate matter,' said Dr Martensen.

'My door is always open,' said Herr Huber.

Dr Martensen lowered himself into the chair on the other side of Herr Huber's desk. 'You will be aware that Dr Schreiber-Ziegler has been investigating our duplicate holdings,' he began.

'Not only am I aware of that, Dr Martensen,' said Herr Huber, 'but I instigated the review myself. It's all to do with shelf space. As a library, we shall soon reach a critical point in our ability to store new material.'

Dr Martensen inclined his head. 'I understand that,' he said. 'But I think it important for discretion and . . .' he hesitated '. . . and, if I may say so, common sense to be shown by those conducting the review.'

This comment could not have been a clearer accusation against Dr Schreiber-Ziegler had it been written up in a formal indictment and delivered by uniformed Officers of the Court. Herr Huber was guarded: this criticism was, after all, being made of his own deputy, and criticism of a deputy might well be considered criticism of a principal under the doctrine of *respondeat superior*.

'I'm not sure that I follow you, Herr Martensen,' Herr Huber said slowly. 'Are you suggesting that too many duplicates are being identified?'

Dr Martensen shifted awkwardly in his seat. 'I'm not saying that, Herr Huber,' he said. 'What concerns me is that there are some duplicates – or indeed multiple copies – that should be kept – because there is a very good reason for keeping them.'

Herr Huber waited, but Dr Martensen did not expand.

'Perhaps you might give me an example,' the Librarian eventually suggested.

Dr Martensen stared at the floor. 'My own modest monograph on Cistercian sign language,' he said. 'We currently have seven copies – or did, shall I say? Dr Schreiber-Ziegler has now removed six of them.'

Herr Huber nodded. 'I see. And why, Herr Martensen, do we need seven copies?' He paused. 'I understand that your monograph is important – I would never question that. And I would never want to see the day when it was not represented in the Library's holdings. But I'm not sure that I see why we should have seven copies – in circumstances when there is pressure on shelf space.'

'What if somebody were to steal it?' said Dr Martensen. 'What then?'

Herr Huber smiled. It was a good-natured smile, as if he were humouring his younger colleague. 'I don't think that is particularly likely, Herr Martensen.'

'Or if more than one person wanted to read it at the same time,' Dr Martensen persisted.

'Again,' said Herr Huber, 'I think that highly unlikely. Indeed, I've never seen anybody read it, let alone two people arguing over a copy.'

There was a brief silence. Then Dr Martensen dropped his bombshell.

'Well,' he began, 'Dr Schreiber-Ziegler also discovered that there are no fewer than twenty-two copies of Professor von Igelfeld's *Portuguese Irregular Verbs* in the library. Twenty-two copies, no less. Of over one thousand pages each.'

Herr Huber caught his breath. This was dangerous territory. 'I am well aware of our strong holding of Professor von Igelfeld's great work,' he said evenly. 'We have all seen the shelf those copies occupy – or shelves, shall I say? – right at the entrance.'

'Occupied – past tense,' muttered Dr Martensen.

Herr Huber froze.

'Dr Schreiber-Ziegler has removed all but one of them,' Dr Martensen went on. 'She has placed them in several large cardboard boxes in the storage room and written on the boxes: *Surplus to requirements. Probably valueless.*'

It was all that Herr Huber could do to stop himself from gasping. After a few moments, when he had recovered, he thanked Dr Martensen for coming to see him, and assured him he would look into the matter – in respect of both publications – and let him know what happened. 'I anticipate that both holdings will be restored to their former size,' he said. 'Leave it with me, Herr Martensen.'

'I know you would be concerned,' Dr Martensen said as he stood up to leave. 'I am all for zeal, but sometimes . . .'

'Yes, yes,' said Herr Huber. 'Excessive zeal is certainly unwelcome in any circumstances.'

Dr Schreiber-Ziegler was at her desk paging through a publisher's catalogue when Herr Huber came into her office. She looked up and smiled at him; so might a conspirator, a *wrecker*, smile innocently at those who, unknown to them, have tumbled to their tricks. No, thought Herr Huber, I shall not be put off in my necessary mission by social superficialities. He therefore did not reciprocate her friendly demeanour.

'What a fine day it is, Herr Librarian,' said Dr Schreiber-Ziegler brightly. 'One might even say *a peach of a day*.'

This immediately wrong-footed Herr Huber, who had always very much wished that his junior staff would address him as Herr Librarian. It was, he knew, an old-fashioned way of speaking, especially in days when people were abandoning even the most basic honorifics and formalities, but it was a mode of address that celebrated the importance of position, and Herr Huber was very much in favour of that.

And yet he had not expected it of Dr Schreiber-Ziegler, of all people – the same Dr Schreiber-Ziegler who had so crudely and provocatively said *phooey* when he had told her of the rules of the Senior Coffee Room. Had she come to her senses? Had there been a Damascene experience that had brought it home to her that if one abandoned formality, then an abyss of uncertainty, of chaos even, opened up before one?

Manners, of course, were imprinted deep in the Librarian's soul, and so he responded to this opening by agreeing politely that it was, in fact, a very fine day. He even went further, pointing out that, if the weather forecast were to be believed, then the following day might be even better. 'Not that I recommend relying entirely on the forecast,' he added, 'but there is often a grain of truth in what they say.'

Dr Schreiber-Ziegler smiled again. 'Speaking of grains, there is a great deal to be said for taking everything *cum grano salis*. I certainly do.'

Herr Huber thought that might be going a bit far – indeed, extremely far – and he wondered whether he had been wrong to lower his guard. A true radical disputed everything, and here was Dr Schreiber-Ziegler expressing scepticism over all matters. Did she extend that attitude of doubt to cover even what she read in the *Frankfurter Allgemeine Zeitung*, that most cautious of newspapers? Herr Huber believed the *FAZ* was right about every subject on which it expressed an opinion, but would Dr Schreiber-Ziegler presume to take what she read even in those columns *cum grano salis*? And what would the editorial director of the newspaper say if he were to hear that there was a deputy librarian at the Institute of Romance Philology who took this critical attitude?

He decided to ignore the point, and move on to the issue

that had brought him to her desk. But, before he was able to do this, Dr Schreiber-Ziegler asked another question that once again put him off his stride.

'And how is your aunt, Herr Huber?' she asked. 'Is everything proceeding smoothly in the nursing home?'

Herr Huber took a moment to compose himself. Then he replied, 'My aunt, Dr Schreiber-Ziegler, is as well as can be expected. And I am happy to report that there have been no incidents of note in the nursing home today.'

'That's good,' said Dr Schreiber-Ziegler. She paused, and then continued, 'I wonder if she talks as much about you as you talk about her.' Then she added, 'Just asking, of course. I wouldn't want to pry.'

Herr Huber frowned. It was very kind of Dr Schreiber-Ziegler to make these enquiries and indeed it was interesting to speculate as to whether his aunt talked about him. He thought that she did, as he had discovered that many members of the nursing home staff seemed to be conversant with developments in the Institute, although he was confident that none of them had ever visited it. Only a day or two ago, one of the nurses had asked after Professor Dr Unterholzer's dog, Walter. This could only be because his aunt, who liked to hear reports of Walter, must have talked to her about it.

'Is it true,' the nurse had asked, 'that the Unterholzers' dog has wheels? Was it born that way, or were these added later?'

The naïveté of the question had tickled Herr Huber, and he had mentioned it to Professor Unterholzer. Unterholzer had looked blank, as if he were struggling to understand the question, and then said simply, 'No dog is born with wheels, Herr Huber – I would have thought that you would have known that.'

'But of course I know that,' Herr Huber had protested, but his retort was unheard by Unterholzer, who had walked away on some pressing business of his own.

Now he answered Dr Schreiber-Ziegler's question. 'I believe that she does talk about my affairs, and those of the Institute,' he said. 'In a positive way, of course. My aunt is not one for tittle-tattle.'

'Of course not,' said Dr Schreiber-Ziegler. 'But who is?' It was a rhetorical question, but she asked it with an enquiring gaze – directed at Herr Huber himself.

Herr Huber ploughed on. 'There's a matter I'd like to raise with you, Dr Schreiber-Ziegler, if I may.'

Dr Schreiber-Ziegler inclined her head. 'I'm all ears, Herr Huber.'

'This shelf-rationalisation that you've been engaged upon,' Herr Huber began. 'I hear that you have moved some very important multiple holdings.'

Dr Schreiber-Ziegler nodded. 'Two, to be precise. I found many duplicates, as well as occasional triplicates and quad-ruplicates, but only two instances of multiple holdings.' She paused, fixing Herr Huber with a disconcertingly direct stare. 'They were ridiculous.'

This brought a sharp intake of breath on Herr Huber's part.

'One was our colleague Martensen's peculiar little pamphlet on Cistercian sign language. I ask you, Herr Huber! Of what possible interest is that? But even if we might want to have a single copy – out of solidarity, so to speak – why on earth would we want to have seven copies? Can you think of a reason? Because, frankly, I can't.'

Herr Huber opened his mouth to reply, but was cut short by Dr Schreiber-Ziegler.

'And then,' she continued, 'there were twenty-two copies of *Portuguese Irregular Verbs*, taking up two long shelves in a prime position within the Library. Twenty-two! And do you know what, Herr Huber? Only two of these had ever been borrowed by a Library user – I looked at the records. Only two. And do you know who was one of those two people to borrow it? Professor Dr Dr von Igelfeld himself – the author of the tome in question.'

Herr Huber raised a finger in protest. 'It does not matter, Dr Schreiber-Ziegler, who borrows a book – the important thing is that it is borrowed.'

'Yes,' retorted Dr Schreiber-Ziegler, 'but why, one might ask, did Professor von Igelfeld choose to borrow a copy of his own book – especially when there are five or six copies of the very same book in his office? I've seen them. There is no shortage of *Portuguese Irregular Verbs* in Professor von Igelfeld's office, I can assure you. So the reason why he borrowed it must have been to have some effect on the statistics. It's an old trick that authors use. They borrow their own books from libraries in order to make their work look more popular than it really is.'

'Professor von Igelfeld would never do such a thing,' protested Herr Huber.

Dr Schreiber-Ziegler shrugged. 'Well, perhaps he forgot that he'd written it, and then he suddenly came across it in the Library and thought, *That looks like an interesting book – I must borrow it.* Perhaps that's what happened, Herr Huber.' She looked challengingly at Herr Huber, and then said, 'Not that one can imagine anybody thinking a book with that title would be interesting.'

Herr Huber was outraged. 'As a matter of fact, it's a very interesting book,' he said. 'And I really don't think you should be talking disparagingly about a colleague's publication.'

'But I thought I was only a deputy librarian,' Dr Schreiber-Ziegler said. 'Am I, in fact, a colleague, with the same rights as the full professors? With an equal right, for instance, to use the Senior Coffee Room? Just to think of an example.'

Herr Huber averted his eyes. 'I'm not prepared to debate academic value with you, Dr Schreiber-Ziegler,' he said. 'I insist that you reinstate Dr Martensen's pamphlets and all the twenty-one volumes of *Portuguese Irregular Verbs* that you have inappropriately removed to a storage area.' He paused, and looked once more at Dr Schreiber-Ziegler, not flinching at her impertinent stare. 'And I would like you to do this *quam primum*.'

Dr Schreiber-Ziegler did not respond immediately. After a

minute or two, though, she rose to her feet to address Herr Huber from the same level. When she did speak, her voice had a cold, steely quality to it. 'I appreciate that you, as Librarian, may instruct me in the exercise of my duties, Herr Huber. But I also understand that I am entitled, under the statutes of the University, to appeal against any instruction you give me to His Magnificence the Rector. I believe that I have that right.'

It would be difficult to imagine a more direct and unambiguous declaration of war. Herr Huber knew that in technical terms she was right – she was entitled to peti-tion the Rector – but he also knew that this power had been used only twice in the past eight years, and on each occasion unsuccessfully. More than that, though: it was the effrontery of Dr Schreiber-Ziegler's assertion that troubled him. Saying *phooey* to senior professors was bad enough; complaining to the Rector amounted to a fundamental challenge to the principles upon which the Institute of Romance Philology had been founded. These were those of independent academic enquiry without fear of interference from the authorities. That was what academic freedom was all about, Herr Huber thought. It was the freedom to do what one liked and not be challenged by people lower down the pecking order who did not like what you did.

Herr Huber drew in his breath. The metaphor of battle suggested itself, but he could think only of Waterloo, Austerlitz and various retreats from Moscow, none of which, he felt, was appropriate for the current situation. So he simply said, 'If that is what you wish to do, then plainly you must do it. But do not delude yourself into thinking that His Magnificence will be able to do the slightest thing for you.'

Dr Schreiber-Ziegler did not appear to be deterred by this warning. 'We'll see,' she said.

'We shall indeed see,' said Herr Huber. '*You'll* see; *I'll* see; we shall *all* see.'

Dr Schreiber-Ziegler gave Herr Huber a curious glance. 'I don't mean this personally, you know,' she said.

Herr Huber stared at her. 'But you're challenging my authority,' he pointed out.

Dr Schreiber-Ziegler laughed. 'Is that what you think it is?'

'Yes,' said Herr Huber. 'I cannot see it as anything other than that.'

Dr Schreiber-Ziegler looked bored. 'Actually, it's far more than that. It's a challenge to outdated patriarchy. It's a questioning of assumptions of superiority made on the slenderest of grounds. It's a knocking on the door of privilege.'

Herr Huber looked confused. 'I don't see what this has got to do with any of that,' he said.

'If you can't see that,' said Dr Schreiber-Ziegler evenly, 'then I'm sorry to say, Herr Huber, that you're part of the problem.'

They looked at one another for several minutes, neither speaking. Herr Huber looked red, and he felt flushed. He wished that he had one of his aunt's pills in his pockets – not the red ones to raise blood pressure, but the small white ones used to lower it. And he suspected, too, that his urate levels were rising, but that was another issue.

He turned on his heels. As he did so, he said to Dr Schreiber-Ziegler, 'Do you know something, Dr Schreiber-Ziegler? If I were to tell the people at the nursing home about this – if I were to relay all that has been said – do you know what their reaction would be? Well, I can tell you: they wouldn't believe it – they simply wouldn't.'

'Do you think I care for one moment about that?' said Dr Schreiber-Ziegler, her voice now on the edge of laughter.

Herr Huber struggled to control himself. 'Oh, you can think *phooey* as much you like,' he said. 'But what if the Rector says *phooey* back to you? Have you thought about that, Dr Schreiber-Ziegler?'

'We'll see,' said Dr Schreiber-Ziegler with a grin.

'We certainly shall,' said Herr Huber. He was rather pleased with his final retort about the Rector saying *phooey*. That will make her think, he told himself.

drei

The Gravest of Emergencies

Herr Huber considered going straight to Professor von Igelfeld to inform him of the unfortunate situation that had arisen in the Library. On subsequent reflection, though, he decided that it might be preferable to resolve the matter without von Igelfeld's ever hearing about it. That would undoubtedly be less traumatic for him, as he was known to be sensitive about his great work and ready to spot any slight to its reputation. To hear that the Library's holdings had been reduced from twenty-two copies to one would be a profound shock for him, and Herr Huber was keen to avoid that if at all possible.

The solution came to him over coffee. The Senior Coffee Room was empty when Herr Huber arrived, apart from Professor Dr Detlev Amadeus Unterholzer, who was seated in his customary chair near the window. Herr Huber helped himself to coffee and made his way to the chair next to Unterholzer's.

Unterholzer looked up sharply as Herr Huber prepared to sit down. 'That chair, Herr Huber,' he said, 'is usually occupied by Professor Dr Dr Prinzel. I'm sure you would not wish to cause any confusion when he arrives.'

'I am aware of that, Herr Unterholzer,' said Herr Huber. 'It's just that I have some grave news to convey to you before the others come.'

A look of concern came over Unterholzer's face. 'Oh, Herr Huber – I'm so sorry. Your aunt . . .'

Unterholzer saw that Herr Huber was shaking his head. 'No, Professor Unterholzer, my aunt is in rude health. This has nothing to do with her. This is an internal Institute matter.'

Unterholzer looked disappointed. 'I see,' he said, glancing at his watch. 'I must keep an eye on the time, Herr Huber – you know how it is.'

Herr Huber assured him that he would be brief, and began an account of Dr Martensen's complaint and of his subsequent conversation with Dr Schreiber-Ziegler. Unterholzer listened attentively, raising an eyebrow when the undignified fate of the extra copies of *Portuguese Irregular Verbs* came to be mentioned. But it was just a raised eyebrow, rather to the surprise of Herr Huber, who faltered at this point.

'You do see the significance of this?' the Librarian asked. 'This is not just any old book – this is *Portuguese Irregular Verbs*.'

Unterholzer made an impatient gesture. 'Oh, I

understand that, Herr Huber,' he said. 'But, to be quite frank, I've often wondered whether we need quite so many copies of our dear colleague's book when my own contribution – and I'm not setting particular store by my work on the imperfect subjunctive, but when that book – which, I might point out – not that I would – has been given such a warm reception – when my own book should be represented in the Library by a single copy? Yes, a single copy, Herr Huber – not that I'm in any way reproaching you over that. That is definitely not my intention – but a single copy . . .'

Herr Huber swallowed hard. 'I very much regret that oversight, Herr Unterholzer. We shall, of course, order some extra copies immediately. This afternoon, in fact.'

Unterholzer seemed appeased by this. 'That would be very wise, Herr Huber. And as to the matter of *Portuguese Irregular Verbs*, I think you would be well advised to keep out of it. A decision has been made, and it is one that will liberate shelf space for other books – including, if I may say so, my own work. The new copies of my book will require shelf space, and now, it appears, Dr Schreiber-Ziegler's sterling work will make that available.'

Herr Huber was far from satisfied, but did not press the matter. Drinking his coffee as quickly as he could, he returned to his office. Seeing that Dr Schreiber-Ziegler was not at her desk, he enquired of his secretary whether she knew where his deputy was. The reply was chilling.

'I received a message from the Rector's office,' she said. 'It said that the Rector would see her immediately if she cared to go round there.'

Herr Huber caught his breath. *The Rector would see her immediately . . .* That was ominous. One might expect a wait of several days, or even weeks, before getting an appointment to see the Rector, but the door had opened immediately for Dr Schreiber-Ziegler. This did not bode at all well, thought Herr Huber, who now began to think that defensive strategies should be prepared. It was always possible that the Rector might decide matters the wrong way, and uphold Dr Schreiber-Ziegler's complaint. That would be a terrible outcome, but, if it occurred, then all the consequences could be laid fairly and squarely at Dr Schreiber-Ziegler's door. She would have to explain to von Igelfeld as to why twenty-one copies of his book were missing – an unenviable task, thought Herr Huber. It would be a painful lesson for her to learn; but most lessons are painful, thought Herr Huber – especially the valuable ones.

Dr Schreiber-Ziegler knocked on Herr Huber's door later that afternoon. Herr Huber had been busy and his mind had been elsewhere; the arrival of Dr Schreiber-Ziegler brought him back to the distinctly uncomfortable present.

Dr Schreiber-Ziegler's tone was jaunty. 'A quick word, Herr Librarian?'

Herr Huber gestured to the chair on the other side of his desk.

'You may recall that I said I was going to speak to the Rector,' said Dr Schreiber-Ziegler. 'Well, I did. Today.'

Herr Huber inclined his head. 'It was your prerogative,' he said. 'And I would never try to stop you from doing that which you are entitled to do, even if it seems like madness . . .'

'Oh, come now, Herr Huber,' said Dr Schreiber-Ziegler. 'This is all a bit of a storm in a teacup, is it not? I wouldn't say that madness comes into it at all.'

'Others may take a different view of that,' Herr Huber retorted. 'These things, you know, are very easily started, but not so readily finished.'

Dr Schreiber-Ziegler shrugged. 'We'll have to agree to differ, then,' she said. 'But I must say, the Rector was most agreeable. He was most attentive to me.'

Herr Huber remained tight-lipped. He did not like the sound of that. He did not see Dr Schreiber-Ziegler as being particularly attractive, but it was always possible that others might find that sort of person appealing – the Rector, for instance.

He waited.

'I told him that there were communication issues here in the Library,' Dr Schreiber-Ziegler continued. 'I said that there did not appear to be any means of resolving misunderstandings.'

Herr Huber found himself tripping up over the word *misunderstandings*. A deliberate demotion of a colleague's book – a work of considerable reputation in Romance philology circles – was that to be considered a *misunder-standing*? If that were the case, then the Napoleonic Wars might equally be described as a *local misunderstanding*. He might have stopped Dr Schreiber-Ziegler there, but she had, anyway, continued.

'He said that what he normally recommended in such cases was a meeting involving his office, the Director of the Office of Personnel, and the Director of the department or institute involved. He said that this normally ironed out any difficulties that had cropped up.'

'I see,' said Herr Huber.

'Then he asked me who the Director of the Institute was.'

Herr Huber's eyes narrowed. Once again they were on perilous ground.

'I replied,' went on Dr Schreiber-Ziegler, 'that, as far as I could tell, there was no Director. Or at least, I said, I have yet to meet anybody occupying such a post.'

Herr Huber sighed. 'We have not had a Director in recent years,' he said. 'It has not been necessary.'

'Well, I can tell you that the Rector won't like that,' said Dr Schreiber-Ziegler. 'He telephoned somebody there and then to check up on who the Director was, and he was given the same answer.'

'We cannot have a meeting involving the Director,' said Herr Huber, 'because we don't have one – and you can't have a meeting with somebody who doesn't exist, Dr Schreiber-Ziegler.'

He said this with an air of triumph, but Dr Schreiber-Ziegler did not seem to be impressed. 'Well, be that as it may, Herr Huber, the Rector said that he would be visiting the Institute shortly to look into the way in which it is run. He said that he couldn't see how an institute could get by without a director. *A ship must have a captain*, is what he said.'

For a few moments, Herr Huber sat quite still. There was nothing he could say to this, he decided, and he would not try. Dr Schreiber-Ziegler had taken a stick, sharpened it with malice, and poked it into the most sensitive target she could find. That, he supposed, was what revolutionaries did. Well, she had better look out, because there were such people as counter-revolutionaries, and they had means at their disposal of fighting back.

He said none of this, of course. Instead, he said, 'Well, I look forward to meeting the Rector and discussing this with him and with my colleagues, Professor Dr Dr von Igelfeld, Professor Dr Unterholzer, and Professor Dr Dr Prinzel – at a joint meeting in the Institute.'

'And me,' said Dr Schreiber-Ziegler.

Herr Huber frowned. 'It will be just the academic staff,' he said.

Dr Schreiber-Ziegler shook her head. 'No, I don't think so, Herr Huber. The Rector very specifically said that I should attend. *Ipse dixit.*'

'He said that, did he?'

'Yes.'

'In that case,' said Herr Huber. 'In that case . . .'

Dr Schreiber-Ziegler finished the sentence for him. 'In that case I shall be there,' she said. And then she added, almost as an afterthought, although it was, in reality, any-thing but, 'I shall be able to tell you what happens at the meeting, Herr Huber, as the Rector didn't say anything about your being invited. Sorry about that.'

With his heart in his mouth, Herr Huber called a meeting of the three professors – and himself – in the Senior Coffee Room. It was a most unusual – even impertinent – thing for a librarian to do, and all three of the professors concluded that only a crisis of the first order of magnitude would justify such a step. Only Unterholzer, however, had any inkling of the reason that might lie behind it, and he remained tight-lipped about it.

'I can't imagine what has possessed Herr Huber to do this,' said von Igelfeld to Unterholzer. 'It must be a most serious matter to warrant a step of this nature.'

More serious than you might imagine, von Igelfeld, thought Unterholzer.

'Do you have any idea what's going on?' von Igelfeld asked.

Unterholzer looked out of the window in a studied way. Eventually he responded, 'There might be some difficulties in the Library. I'm not sure that Herr Huber and that new deputy of his have hit it off. In fact, I fear they may not have done so at all.'

'That has nothing to do with us,' said von Igelfeld. 'Library matters are for librarians to sort out, and they cannot expect professors to get involved. You and I have bigger fish to fry, Herr Unterholzer.'

'Possibly,' said Unterholzer.

When they were all assembled, Herr Huber cleared his throat and began. 'I am very sorry to be eating into your time in this way,' he said. 'But we are faced with an emergency of which I felt I must inform you without delay.'

The eyes of the three professors were fixed on him. Rarely, if ever, had Herr Huber commanded such attention.

'I am told that we are to receive a visit from His Magnificence the Rector.'

Nobody stirred. Nobody uttered a word.

'I am further told,' Herr Huber went on, 'that he intends to investigate the governance of the Institute.'

If silence had greeted his opening announcement, his audience now made up for that. 'Ridiculous!' muttered Prinzel. 'Absurd.'

'What governance?' exclaimed von Igelfeld.

'Interference,' said Unterholzer. 'If he thinks he can investigate us, then why shouldn't we investigate him?'

'What brought this about, Herr Huber?' demanded Prinzel.

Herr Huber paled. He had wanted to avoid mentioning *Portuguese Irregular Verbs*, but now it seemed that disclosure of the *casus belli* might be inevitable.

'There might have been a disagreement between me and my new deputy, Dr Schreiber-Ziegler,' he said.

'Over what?' asked Prinzel.

Herr Huber avoided looking at von Igelfeld. 'Over the pruning of multiple copies of certain titles in the Library.'

Von Igelfeld looked up sharply. 'Which multiple copies?' he snapped.

Herr Huber made a careless gesture with his right hand. 'Oh, you know how it is – this and that.'

'But we do not have many multiple copies,' said Prinzel. 'The only title I know of in the Library that is represented multiple times is . . . *Portuguese Irregular Verbs.*'

This brought complete silence, as all eyes turned to von Igelfeld.

'There are, what, twenty-two copies of that in the Library, are there not?' asked Prinzel.

'No longer,' said Unterholzer. 'In fact, as of two days ago, there is only one. The rest are in a box in the store-room marked . . . now what did the label say? Oh, yes, I remember now: *probably valueless*. That's what it said: *probably valueless.*'

Von Igelfeld was staring at the floor. He, too, had paled.

'That was written by Dr Schreiber-Ziegler,' Herr Huber said hurriedly. 'I have taken steps to remove it.'

Unterholzer raised a finger. 'Mind you,' he said, 'although nobody in their right mind would concur with that thoroughly inaccurate description, there is an interesting point here. Do we need so many copies of one book? I only ask because my own work is represented by a single copy – currently – and I've been wondering whether there is any point to having so many copies of *Portuguese Irregular Verbs*.'

'That is a matter of opinion, Herr Unterholzer,' snapped von Igelfeld. 'I can't imagine, though, that you are suggesting scholarly equivalence here. There might be reasons why there is only one copy of your book in the Library.'

Unterholzer bit his lip. 'Perhaps the reason is that I didn't coerce the Librarian into buying multiple copies. Unlike some, if I may say so, Herr von Igelfeld.'

It was at this point that Prinzel intervened. 'I really don't think this is the time for recrimination,' he said, casting a disapproving glance in Unterholzer's direction. 'We must decide what to do should the Rector come to the Institute.'

'Which is going to happen,' Herr Huber assured them.

'So, what do we do?' asked Prinzel. 'What if he finds fault with the way we run things here? What view will he take of our Senior Coffee Room, for instance? Are we to be compelled to open it to students – or even the public at large?'

Von Igelfeld thought this was a *reductio ad absurdum*. 'That's highly unlikely, Herr Prinzel,' he said, 'even in these debased days.'

'I wouldn't be so sure,' counselled Unterholzer. 'I was reading about a new doctrine of compulsory anti-elitism the other day. People are being compelled to invite their neighbours into their houses. It's a very popular notion – people don't approve of elitism.'

'Elitism?' asked von Igelfeld. 'What has that got to do with us?'

Prinzel tapped the table. 'We must have a strategy,' he said. 'We must think very carefully about this.'

They looked at one another. The external threat had united them now, and thoughts of rivalry over whose books were best represented in the Library had been replaced by a mutual concern to ensure that the work they all cherished so much could be protected from the interference of revolutionaries like Dr Schreiber-Ziegler, and from officious busybodies like the Rector. There were other enemies too, vague and uncertain, enemies without a name, circling in the darkness, ready to pounce.

vier

His Magnificence the Rector

The Rector lost little time in arranging his visit to the Institute. The following morning at ten o'clock, a large black Mercedes-Benz drew up in front of the Institute building. The car was flying the flag of the University of Regensburg and was driven by a chauffeur in a pale grey uniform. When the chauffeur stepped out smartly to open one of the rear passenger doors, out of the car there appeared the figure of the Rector, Professor Ludwig-Otto Dietrich, and his Director of Personnel, Herr Ferdinand Uber-Huber. The Rector was a tall, powerfully built man in his early sixties; Herr Uber-Huber was an only marginally less impressive man, with a slightly angled mouth – a legacy of an early minor attack of Bell's palsy.

The Rector had a brief word with his driver before he and Herr Uber-Huber bounded up the steps that led to the Institute's front door.

'It looks as though we have a welcoming committee,'

said the Rector, pointing through the glass door at the three professors and Dr Schreiber-Ziegler waiting for them inside. 'And there's that rather attractive librarian, Dr Schreiber-Ziegler – I told you about her, I think. She's probably the only progressive force in this place. One to watch, I'd say.'

'They keep to themselves, this department,' said Herr Uber-Huber. 'They're ripe for reform, I'd say.'

'Sometimes the best sort of reform is abolition,' said the Rector, with a smile. 'Not that they'd like that, I suspect.'

Von Igelfeld welcomed them as they went into the entrance hall. 'Your Magnificence,' he said, 'this is a great honour for the Institute.'

The Rector bowed. 'I've been meaning to come for years, but somehow I never got round to it.'

'Better late than never,' said von Igelfeld.

This witticism relieved the tension, and introductions were made in a friendly manner.

'And here we have the Librarian,' said the Rector as Dr Schreiber-Ziegler stepped forward to shake his hand.

'Deputy Librarian,' said Dr Schreiber-Ziegler quickly. 'The Librarian is Herr Huber.'

'Of course,' said the Rector. And then, turning to Herr Uber-Huber, he said, 'Another Huber, you see, Herr Uber-Huber. Bavaria's teeming with people of your name.'

'Hubers, yes,' said Herr Uber-Huber. 'But not so many Uber-Hubers, I think.'

'An important distinction, that,' said the Rector. 'Tell me, Herr Uber-Huber – are there any Unter-Hubers, as far as you know?'

Herr Uber-Huber shook his head. 'I would say that Huber is the equivalent of Unter-Huber.'

Dr Schreiber-Ziegler laughed. 'That's very funny,' she said.

'Indeed,' said the Rector, casting an appreciative glance at Dr Schreiber-Ziegler. 'But perhaps we should start our little meeting. Do you have a coffee room, Dr Schreiber-Ziegler? Perhaps we could conduct our meeting there.'

Dr Schreiber-Ziegler grinned. 'Do *I* have a coffee room? No, *I* do not, but some of my colleagues do.'

The Rector looked confused. 'You mean . . .'

'I mean, I'm not permitted to have coffee in the Senior Coffee Room. Apparently there is some ancient rule to that effect.'

The Rector frowned. 'But that is not in the spirit of equality that we promote at this university,' he said. 'I'm sure that this can be addressed.'

'That would be nice,' said Dr Schreiber-Ziegler. 'And there may be other ancient rules that could be reconsidered in due course.'

'Undoubtedly,' said Herr Uber-Huber. 'It's amazing what one uncovers once one begins to investigate. People who say that all dinosaurs are extinct have got it wrong, I fear.'

Von Igelfeld's expression had been growing steadily grimmer. Now he said, 'I do not see what this conversation has to do with the affairs of the Institute. Coffee rooms, dinosaurs – these are very interesting topics, but they throw no light on anything very much.'

The Rector nodded. 'You're right, Herr von . . . von . . .'

'Igelfeld,' said von Igelfeld.

'Yes, Herr von Igelfeld. You're right in saying that minor matters should not be our main concern – but they do reveal something about the underlying *culture* of a place – about how non-elitist it is, for example; how relevant it is to the needs of our times; how safe an environment – that sort of thing.'

They made their way to the Senior Coffee Room, where they seated themselves and began their meeting – or *inquisition*, as von Igelfeld was later to describe it.

'It is very important to recognise the democratic principle in academic structures,' began the Rector. 'And so I thought we might begin by enquiring how you elect your Director.'

There was complete silence. Outside, the bells of the local church chimed the hour. Then silence returned.

'I see,' said Herr Uber-Huber. 'Are we to take it, then, that you do not have elections?'

'Or a Director?' added the Rector.

Glances were exchanged. 'We operate by consensus,' said Prinzel eventually.

'That's right,' said von Igelfeld. 'It often falls to me to identify the most suitable policy, and then we agree it.'

The silence that followed this was a distinctly chilly one.

'And consultation?' asked the Rector. 'How do you consult?'

Von Igelfeld was brisk. 'That is rarely necessary,' he said. 'I know intuitively what my dear colleagues Prinzel and Unterholzer will think on any subject – and they know that same of me.'

The Rector's eyes widened.

'You see,' muttered Dr Schreiber-Ziegler, *sotto voce* but loud enough for Herr Uber-Huber to hear her.

'Dr Schreiber-Ziegler said *you see*,' Herr Uber-Huber whispered to the Rector.

'And so I do,' muttered the Rector.

'I think that went rather well,' von Igelfeld observed to Prinzel later that day. 'What is that expression . . . *he came to mock and stayed to pray?*'

Prinzel was not so sanguine. 'It's true he listened,' he said, 'but there's a difference between listening and agreeing – sometimes quite a substantial difference, in fact.'

'I confidently predict we've heard the last of the Rector,' von Igelfeld insisted.

'We shall see,' said Prinzel, doubtfully.

'One shouldn't encourage people like that,' said von Igelfeld. 'You have to be firm with them. Stamp your authority on a meeting at the outset. Show that you're not a pushover. It's the only language they understand.'

'Yes,' said Prinzel, but with no conviction. This was His Magnificence the Rector to whom von Igelfeld was referring – not some inconsequential university bureaucrat, like Herr Uber-Huber.

And Prinzel's misgivings were to prove well founded. The following day a letter was sent from the office of Herr Uber-Huber, setting out the governance structure that the Rector had authorised him to implement. This letter was received by the three professors, but also by the Librarian and by Dr Schreiber-Ziegler, whose name, everybody noticed, led all the others on the distribution list.

'Since when,' Prinzel asked, 'did *deputy* librarians—'

'Or *any* librarian,' interjected Unterholzer.

'Since when,' Prinzel continued, 'did librarians precede professors in correspondence?'

'Since today, it would seem,' said von Igelfeld, shaking his head in disbelief.

'The world has changed,' observed Unterholzer. 'The world has become topsy-turvy.'

They absorbed the content of the letter in mute disbelief. The Rector, announced Herr Uber-Huber, was firm in his intention of imposing a transparent and responsive system of governance for all university departments. To this end, the Institute would be required to elect a Director from among the academic *and library* staff, this Director holding office for three years, with the possibility of extension for a further two years. Each member of the academic and library staff at or above the rank of deputy librarian was entitled to vote and to stand for the post of Director.

'Well, it could have been worse, I suppose,' said Unterholzer. 'He might have extended the franchise to the likes of Martensen or the Müllers. At least that hasn't happened.'

'Small consolation,' said Prinzel.

Von Igelfeld wondered whether they might mount a legal challenge to the Rector's ruling.

'I doubt it,' said Prinzel. 'People like Herr Uber-Huber will have gone into that pretty thoroughly, I imagine. You know what these bureaucrats are like – they're very careful about covering themselves.'

'What about the European Court of Human Rights?' asked von Igelfeld. 'This is just the sort of thing they were set up to deal with.'

Again, Prinzel was doubtful. 'Those sorts of challenges take years,' he said. 'Even in a meritorious case like this. And litigation is immensely expensive.'

Unterholzer nodded sadly. 'I had an uncle who was almost ruined by a court case. All over a crop of potatoes.'

Von Igelfeld looked pained. If one had potatoes in the family, you would think one would keep them there – in the background – rather than drawing attention to them.

'That's true,' he said. 'Lawyers are expensive, and with the way things are, it's not at all clear one would get a fair hearing. The courts are biased against people like us.'

Unterholzer looked puzzled. 'People like us, Herr von Igelfeld?'

'Upholders of certain unchanging values,' von Igelfeld explained. 'Defenders of academic freedom.'

'Safeguarders of standards,' added Prinzel.

'That too,' agreed von Igelfeld.

'So, we have no choice but to comply?' asked Unterholzer.

'That appears to be the case,' said von Igelfeld. 'Which suggests that we make a plan to ensure that this so-called election goes the way we want it to.'

'Which is?' asked Unterholzer.

There was a short period of silence. Then von Igelfeld said, 'We need to ensure that, whoever gets the directorship, it's not Herr Huber or Dr Schreiber-Ziegler.'

'You put it somewhat bluntly,' said Prinzel.

'Well,' challenged von Igelfeld, 'would *you* like either of them to be elected Director?'

Prinzel did not answer immediately, and so von Igelfeld repeated his question. 'Would you?' he asked.

Prinzel shook his head. 'Can you imagine it? If she got the post, she'd be in here drinking coffee all day – we could hardly exclude the Director of the Institute from the Senior Coffee Room.'

'We could try,' said Unterholzer.

Von Igelfeld shook his head. 'You have to be realistic,' he said. 'If we tried that – tempting though it undoubtedly is – we'd get Herr Uber-Huber down here in an instant, lecturing us on anti-elitism, transparency, democracy, re-cycling – the lot.'

'And that would be intolerable,' said Prinzel. 'No, I think Herr von Igelfeld is right. We would have to let her into the Senior Coffee Room if she were to get the post.'

'Which she never will,' said Unterholzer. 'Not if we decide to vote as a bloc.'

'Exactly,' said von Igelfeld. 'So, all we have to do is to decide which one of us three will be the candidate. Then we shall vote for him. It wouldn't matter, then, how poor Herr Huber and Dr Schreiber-Ziegler voted – it would be 3-2 in favour of our candidate.'

Prinzel thought of something. 'Of course, we don't really have any idea of how Herr Huber would vote, do we? He wouldn't necessarily vote for Dr Schreiber-Ziegler just because they're both librarians. I get the impression he's wary of her.'

'As well he might be,' said Unterholzer. 'She's a very dangerous woman, that. Very.'

Prinzel smiled. 'Imagine if Herr Huber were to be elected,' he said. 'I'm not saying it's likely to happen – I'm certainly not saying that. But just imagine.'

'He might give an annual Director's Lecture,' said von Igelfeld. 'Many directors do that. But they – these other directors – don't talk about their aunts in their lectures. Herr Huber would, I think. Leopards don't change their spots just because they've been elected directors.'

'And he'd send us endless memos,' said Prinzel. 'You know how he loves to send a memo – usually about nothing.'

Unterholzer laughed. 'His memos would be headed: *Re nothing.*'

'We shouldn't laugh about things that could just happen,' said Prinzel. 'Remember that we are in grave danger.'

'Yes,' said von Igelfeld. 'And we need to reach an agreement on strategy. I might start the ball rolling, if I may, by saying that I would be happy to stand for the post of Director.'

Nobody said anything for a good minute. Then Prinzel said, 'I wouldn't mind either.'

Von Igelfeld frowned. 'Wouldn't mind what, Herr Prinzel? Wouldn't mind it if I – that is Professor Dr Dr von Igelfeld – stood, or wouldn't mind . . .' His voice trailed away – he did not want to give voice to the possibility that somebody else might want to secure the post that was so rightfully his.

'I wouldn't mind standing for the post of Director,' said Prinzel.

Von Igelfeld fixed Prinzel with a piercing stare. 'I've already indicated my interest,' he said coldly. 'My nomination was put in first, if I may say so.'

Unterholzer opened his mouth to object, but his objection was anticipated by Prinzel, who said, 'You only indicated your candidature a minute or so ago. You have no prior right, Herr von Igelfeld.'

Von Igelfeld bit his lip. 'I'm surprised that you would take that tone, Herr Prinzel. Had it been you to indicate candidature first, I would without question have supported you and would not have dreamed of proposing myself. But perhaps that's just me – I fully understand that not everybody sees things the same way as I do.'

Unterholzer cleared his throat. 'Excuse me, dear colleagues,' he began. 'It is very important that we do not allow disagreements to imperil our unity.' He looked severely at Prinzel, who looked away pointedly. 'For this reason, I am proposing to back Herr von Igelfeld on the grounds of seniority. That means that he would get at least two votes. Now, if I were in your position, Herr Prinzel, I would withdraw your candidature gracefully and transfer your support to Herr von Igelfeld.'

Von Igelfeld, though gratified by this support, was slightly surprised at the quarter from which it came. He and Unterholzer had always been rivals, although Unterholzer had never been the remotest threat to him. In circumstances such as those now prevailing, he would have imagined that it would be Unterholzer who would propose himself for the post of Director, and Prinzel who would have come up with the unity-based counter-proposal. But it had been the other way round. Which just went to show, von Igelfeld thought, that in politics there was no telling in which way the cards would play out.

Prinzel clearly resented Unterholzer's move, but now

gave a grudging assent to the proposal. 'I'm not one to rock the boat,' he said. 'And if this is what you want, Herr Unterholzer, I'm prepared to withdraw.'

'Good,' said Unterholzer quickly. 'In that case, we are all of one mind. Herr von Igelfeld's will be the name that we all inscribe on our voting papers. Is that agreed?'

Von Igelfeld sought clarification on one matter. 'Am I to vote for myself?' he asked.

Unterholzer nodded. 'I know how modest you are, Herr von Igelfeld, but it will indeed be necessary for you to cast your vote for yourself. Otherwise the other side could slip in by default – or it could be a draw.' He paused. 'Their candidate might get two votes, and then there would be the two votes cast by Professor Prinzel and myself, and your vote would not break any deadlock, you see. So you have to vote for yourself – there is no alternative.'

Von Igelfeld inclined his head. Politics was a very pushy business, he thought, with very little room for modesty or reticence. That was the world into which the Rector, with his ill-conceived intervention, was now propelling them – a world of factionalism and self-promotion, a world that was completely antipathetic to the refined atmosphere of scholarship that had hitherto prevailed in the Institute. Such was the modern world, he told himself; such was the decline of all the things he had believed in from the very beginning of his academic career. What would Zimmermann make of this? he asked himself – Zimmermann, who stood for the old academic values and standards and who was worth any number of Rectors and Herr Uber-Hubers. He would write to him, he decided, and tell him all about it. He would write to him once he was Director and had had new notepaper printed to reflect the change in his status.

That was the end of the discussion, and the three professors returned, with some relief, to their offices and to their research. Nothing more was said about Herr Uber-Huber's letter that day, but the following morning the matter arose again when another letter was received from that same gentleman. In this, he announced the day of the election of the Director, which was to take place a full month later. This was rather a long time away, they all thought, although it happened to suit von Igelfeld rather well. He had this very week received an invitation from All Souls College, Oxford, to take up a short-term Visiting Fellowship, the duration of which was, conveniently, three weeks.

'You may take up the Fellowship whenever you wish,' wrote the Deputy Warden-Substitute (Visiting Fellowships), Dr Mottle. 'We are very flexible.'

Von Igelfeld wrote back immediately. 'I shall arrive in Oxford next week,' he said. 'I shall be travelling by way of London, and will present myself at the College next Tuesday afternoon at two p.m. I take it that this is acceptable to you.'

'Good heavens,' said Dr Mottle to his secretary. 'Have you seen this message from that peculiar German that Professor

Plowson has put up for a Visiting Fellowship? Next Tuesday, he says. Can you believe it?'

'Very odd people, the Germans,' said his secretary. 'Frightfully efficient.'

'I know,' said Dr Mottle. 'But really . . .' He paused. 'Has Plowson hatched up some sort of agenda with this German person? You know how I don't trust him.'

'Nobody does,' said the secretary. 'And an agenda? More or less certainly. Everything Professor Plowson does is done according to a concealed agenda.'

'Ghastly man,' said Dr Mottle, with a sigh. 'I wish somebody would kill him.' But then he relented. 'I don't mean that, of course.'

'Drill through his tongue?' suggested the secretary. 'That was a punishment they used in the time of Charles I. It was a punishment for blasphemy.'

'A bit extreme,' said Dr Mottle. 'But some form of humiliation would be perfect.' He thought of something. 'You know what we did when I was at school?' he asked. 'We used to punish unpopular boys by pinning a notice on their back saying *Kick Me*. Somebody would then come along and give the poor chap a great kick. It was terribly childish – but immensely satisfying.'

'Boys will be boys, Dr Mottle,' said the secretary, with a smile.

'Oh, yes,' he said. 'Still, I suppose we'd better make arrangements for this . . .' He looked at a piece of paper he was holding. 'For this Professor von Igelfeld. He'll need a room. Is there anything vacant at present?'

'There's that room that was occupied by that professor from Harvard. It's been repaired now, I believe.'

'That's it, then,' said Dr Mottle. He looked thoughtful. 'Plowson's up to something,' he said. 'And this von Igelfeld character will be in it up to his neck – absolutely definitely, without the remotest shadow of doubt.'

Dr Mottle looked at his secretary. 'Why is the world so complicated, Mrs Evans? Why can't people co-operate with one another without plotting and scheming and arguing about this that and the next thing?'

Mrs Evans sighed. She had recently completed an Open University unit in socio-biology and the answer came to her readily. 'Because of the nature of man, Dr Mottle,' she said. 'We are a competitive species. We compete for food; we compete for territory; we compete for mates. Competition is at the very heart of our existence.' She paused. 'And change. They say we must be competitive and, in order to be competitive, we must embrace change.'

She looked at Dr Mottle. He was the wrong shape for the modern age. Everything about him was wrong: he was a man, first of all, which disqualified him from being modern; he was ... Oh, everything about him was wrong. But she admired him so much. She would do anything for him – anything. She was happily married – there was Mr Evans at home, a thin and rather taciturn man interested in tropical fish, and she had had three children by him, two of whom were microbiologists and were doing well. They were happy, but if Dr Mottle were to declare himself suddenly and invite her to go to Costa Rica with him, she would do so like a shot.

She stared out of the window. 'Change,' she said. 'These people . . .' and here she waved a hand in the general direction of London, over an hour away on the train '. . . these people say that we're elitist and out of touch. With whom? With whom are we out of touch, Dr Mottle?'

'People are out of touch with us,' he said. 'That's the real problem, Mrs Evans.'

'They want us to be enthusiastic about change. They say that change is good in itself.'

Dr Mottle buried his head in his hands, in a gesture of despair. 'Oh, for stasis,' he said. 'Oh, to go out on to the High Street there and discover that nothing has changed. Or, even better, to find that things have actually gone in reverse. Wouldn't that be marvellous, Mrs Evans? Wouldn't it be a wonderful thing to go out on to the street and discover that all the tourists had gone away and that it was just well-behaved undergraduates and a few furtive dons?'

'Oh, it would, Dr Mottle. And to see that people were driving Morris Minors rather than these flashy Korean cars or whatever it is they drive nowadays. And bicycles – people would still be riding bicycles with proper brakes and, at the most, three gears, only two of which would work!'

Dr Mottle closed his eyes in ecstasy. 'A Sturmey-Archer three-speed – made in Britain! Such a pleasure. And cycle clips, Mrs Evans, that one could clip about one's shins to avoid one's trouser legs being caught up in the chain. And Evensong in one of the College chapels, with a College chaplain who wears old brogues that his father wore when he was a rector in some dim village in Gloucestershire. And afterwards, in a pub with low ceilings and warm beer, where you'd have to be careful not to sit too close to the dartboard.'

Mrs Evans shared Dr Mottle's delight, but now she sounded a note of caution. 'We have so many enemies, Dr Mottle – so many people who want to take away the few vestiges that remain of that life.'

'Don't I know it, Mrs Evans,' he exclaimed. 'We shall have to fight back. We shall have to resist the tide of vulgarity that threatens to inundate us all.'

'We shall indeed, Dr Mottle. But how?'

'By defeating Plowson,' Dr Mottle answered. 'He is the most immediate threat.'

'But how do we do that?'

Dr Mottle shook his head. 'I have absolutely no idea, Mrs Evans, but we shall have to try.'

He seemed lost in thought for a moment. Then he turned to the secretary.

'Something's occurred to me, Mrs Evans. This German who's coming next week, this Fritz . . .'

'Professor Moritz-Maria von Igelfeld,' said Mrs Evans. 'I don't think we call them Fritzes any longer.'

'Really? Yes, him. He's here at Plowson's instigation, isn't he? So he might just be our route into the Plowson camp, so to speak.'

Mrs Evans did not reply immediately. But then a smile spread slowly across her face. 'Wicked Dr Mottle!' she said, shaking a finger at him.

Dr Mottle winked. 'In the cause of the just, Mrs Evans, no measures are wicked. *Inter arma silent leges*, as they say.'

'Grotius would not have agreed,' said Mrs Evans primly.

'Grotius would not have approved of Plowson,' Dr Mottle retorted.

Mrs Evans looked at Dr Mottle admiringly. What a man! she thought. Here was a man who knew who Grotius was. Here was a man who happened to be a world authority on early civilisations of the Indus valley, who would probably be the first to decipher one of the world's last undeciphered scripts, the script of the ancient Harappan; here was a man who had represented England in croquet on three international tours, including on that extraordinary occasion when the Irish team was found to have been on steroids and was disqualified. And this man, for all his accomplishments and promises, had to waste his time fending off sniping attacks from people like Plowson, who was a simple geographer who spent his days going on about contour lines and patterns of settlement – when he wasn't plotting, of course, against the College authorities.

'I'm sure you're right,' said Mrs Evans. 'Professor von Igelfeld may prove very useful.'

'Even if not a *useful idiot*,' muttered Dr Mottle. 'To paraphrase Uncle Joe.'

Mrs Evans gave a little shiver of pleasure. Stalin was so masterful. She knew he had been a tyrant, but there was something about tyrants that was so masculine; for this was the same Mrs Evans who had once dreamed that she was sharing a bath with Saddam Hussein. She had been so ashamed of that dream, and had confessed it to nobody until finally, when undergoing a brief period of psycho-analysis, she had told her analyst about it. He had simply noted it down in his book, passing no comment, until she had said, 'I feel so embarrassed to be telling you this.' And he had simply said, 'I've heard worse, you know. Not that I should use the word *worse*. I'm not passing judgement on your dream. All that I would say, if you were to press me, is that Saddam Hussein is an archetypal male presence. He is a cipher – no more. You must not worry about this dream.'

Dr Mottle was watching her. 'Useful idiots were people like the Webbs,' he said. 'They went to the Soviet Union and . . .'

Mrs Evans interrupted him. 'I know all about that, Dr Mottle.' She resented his assumption that as a mere secretary she would not know these things. She knew a lot – far more than some of the young dons, who were very limited in what they knew about the world. But he was Dr Mottle, and she would forgive him; she would forgive him anything.

'Of course you do, Mrs Evans.'

She would just make sure that he knew that she knew. 'The useful idiots,' she said, 'went to the Soviet Union and were thoroughly duped. They were given very select-ive tours – of the bits that actually functioned – and then returned full of praise. The same applied to that American journalist Lincoln Steffens, and his wife. He said, *I have seen the future – and it works.* How could people possibly have been so naïve?'

'Never underestimate the ignorance or naïvety of others,' said Dr Mottle. 'That should be one's starting point, I think.'

fünf

At All Souls

Dr Andrea Schneeweiss looked out of the window of her room in All Souls College. In the quad below, two scholarly-looking middle-aged men, clad in brown tweeds, were walking backwards and forwards, deep in discussion. She was intrigued: Andrea had been in Oxford for almost ten weeks, and felt that she understood less about this curious city and its opaque university now than she had when she had arrived. This, of course, made no sense, and she knew it. What had happened was that her preconceptions, which she had misinterpreted as understanding but which were really nothing of the sort, had slowly unravelled. But she was positive in her outlook – a sunny and forward-looking person, as one of her friends described her: one who embraces the world with passion and tenacity.

Dr Schneeweiss was a graduate of the University of Pittsburgh, where she had obtained her undergraduate degree, and of Columbia, from which she held a doctorate.

Columbia had been followed by a two-year spell at Notre Dame, where she held the prestigious Wallace Brabant Post-Doctoral Fellowship in Romance linguistics. That, like all post-doctoral fellowships, had come to an end, and she had been obliged to cast a wide net in search of an associate professorship that would take her one step further up the academic ladder. The rungs of that ladder, as all aspiring scholars discover, are both widely separated and frequently greased, and a long reach, along with grim determination, is required to haul oneself up to the dizzy heights of a tenured Chair.

It was pure chance that had led her to Oxford. All Souls College, finding its investments for the year in an unexpectedly strong position, had decided to advertise at short notice a three-month Visiting Fellowship in linguistics. Dr Schneeweiss had applied and, on the strength of a glowing reference from her professor at Notre Dame, she had been appointed to the Fellowship. That reference, which described her as one of the most impressive young scholars to have emerged in the last decade, went on to suggest that, if Oxford was looking for the next Noam Chomsky, then they need look no further – here she was.

Such praise might sound alarm bells, and might even prompt the conclusion that the candidate had written the reference herself – something that has been known to occur from time to time, just as Walter Scott was believed to have reviewed his own books. This was not the case: the extremely enthusiastic tone of the recommendation was a result of her referee's desire to get rid of Dr Schneeweiss by any means, and what better way of doing so than to recommend her for a Fellowship in another country?

It was not that Dr Schneeweiss was unpromising. She had already published four papers in reputable journals and had signed a contract with Princeton University Press for a monograph that was on the point of completion. Her four papers had been well received, and were registering high scores in the Humanities Citation Index. Her second paper, 'Vowel shifts in medieval Spanish: a re-assessment', had been quoted in seventy-three other papers, and her most recent, jointly authored paper, 'Seventeenth-century sources of Spanish agricultural terminology', had been short-listed for the Annenberg Essay Prize. By any standards, Dr Schneeweiss would be a strong candidate for a tenure-track position at a reputable university – but only – and this was an important qualification – in normal times. And unfortunately times were not normal: the sluggish performance of the economy had imposed financial constraints on many universities, with the result that academic posts, particularly in the more recondite areas of the humanities, were few and far between. And there were reasons why, even if a few posts were to open up, Dr Schneeweiss would find it hard to succeed. This had nothing to do with academic ability, but had a great deal to do with Dr Schneeweiss's enthusiastic manner. Dr Schneeweiss exhausted people.

It was while she was at Notre Dame that Dr Schneeweiss had first come across a copy of *Portuguese Irregular Verbs*. Von Igelfeld's important *opus* had been mentioned in a lecture given by a visiting professor, Professor P. D. F. Williamson of Louisiana State University in Baton Rouge, Louisiana. Professor Williamson had referred to the book in passing, suggesting that any member of the audience who wished to understand the evolution of contemporary Portuguese verb forms should start by reading von Igelfeld's book. 'If you want to understand the changing morphology of the language at certain critical points,' he said, 'then you must start with von Igelfeld.'

Her interest piqued, Dr Schneeweiss had found a copy in the University Library and had taken it back to her apartment to peruse its twelve hundred pages in peace. Her reaction had been immediate – and overwhelming. If Keats could convey intellectual and aesthetic awe in his 'On First Looking into Chapman's Homer', then Dr Schneeweiss might write in a similar vein after her first foray into *Portuguese Irregular Verbs*. What impressed her was the sheer range of the book, and the ease with which von Igelfeld moved between historical epochs. She was taken, too, by the way in which the evidence was marshalled, leading the reader to von Igelfeld's conclusions in such a way that disagreement would be futile. This was scholarship of dimensions that Dr Schneeweiss had never before seen. It was cogent; it was meticulous; it was masterful. *Portuguese*

Irregular Verbs was, in Dr Schneeweiss's view, the definitive work of Romance linguistic scholarship. If she could write something one third as good as this, she told herself, she would count herself lucky.

Dr Schneeweiss read *Portuguese Irregular Verbs* from cover to cover, not knowing – and nobody knew this – that she was only person in the world to have done so – apart from the author himself, of course. Prinzel *claimed* to have read the entire book, but even von Igelfeld, for whose benefit the claim was made, was doubtful as to its veracity. 'It's kind of Professor Prinzel to say that he has read my book in its entirety,' von Igelfeld once said. 'But the fact of the matter, I'm sorry to say, is that he hasn't.'

Dr Schneeweiss was particularly interested in what *Portuguese Irregular Verbs* had to say about the subjunctive, which was one of the main areas in which she worked. She had a special theory about the subjunctive, and had developed this in several published letters to the better-known linguistic journals. She had long believed – and, she thought, established in her own work – that there was a form of the subjunctive mood that expressed what she described as *attenuated hypotheticality*. This arose when the possibility to which the subjunctive verb referred – as in *if you were to decide* – is an unlikely rather than a merely *possible* possibility. This form would be used, then, to express a remote chance – something that as likely as not would not materialise.

Theoretically, one might imagine a language that allowed for such a construction, but what evidence did Dr Schneeweiss have to support her supposition? This was the point at which her position became questionable. Her main piece of evidence, first propounded at a conference in Bloomington, Indiana, was a text she had come across in a minor Dravidian language where an unusual form of the subjunctive mood of the verb *to attack* seemed capable of this reading. Her claims, however, were disputed by more than one expert in the language in question; these critics seemed united in thinking that the text upon which Dr Schneeweiss based her argument was, in fact, riddled with misprints and typographical corruptions, of which the so-called attenuated subjunctive was an example. 'You cannot base a theory on a misprint,' observed one of her critics. 'There is no headway to be made here – none.'

Undeterred, Dr Schneeweiss proposed her theory at every opportunity, even taking to calling the verb mood in question the *Schneeweiss Subjunctive*. Eponymous pretension can always be calculated to give rise to opposition, especially when its proponent is as tenacious and as obsessive as Dr Schneeweiss. When the news came through that she had been awarded a Visiting Fellowship at All Souls, the relief of her colleagues at Notre Dame was palpable. 'We wish Dr Schneeweiss a conspicuously successful career,' said the Head of Department. 'But not here.'

Having bought a private copy of *Portuguese Irregular*

Verbs – one of only three sold that year, the other two having been mistakenly ordered for its phrase-book section by the travel bookstore at Munich Airport – Dr Schneeweiss had embarked upon a second reading of the tome, annotating it here and there in the margins as she went along. These annotations were, without exception, positive, stating *Precisely* or *Confirmed by the direct Italian equivalent*, or some other similar endorsement.

Now, as she gazed out of her window and into the quad below, Dr Schneeweiss was reflecting on the extraordinarily exciting news that she had received that morning from Dr Mottle.

'You might be interested to hear that we're expecting somebody else in your field, Dr Schneeweiss,' he had said.

Dr Schneeweiss had replied in a non-committal way. Oxford was full of people she did not know and even she, with her open and sunny manner, found it a little daunting at times.

'Yes,' Dr Mottle continued. 'A Professor Moritz-Maria von Igelfeld will be arriving this afternoon. He's from Regensburg – you may have heard of him.'

Dr Schneeweiss gasped. 'Von Igelfeld?'

Dr Mottle nodded. 'Yes, von Igelfeld. He's the author of a rather impressive work of scholarship, actually, *Portuguese Constipated Verbs*.'

'*Irregular Verbs*,' corrected Dr Schneeweiss.

Dr Mottle looked puzzled. 'Yes, that's what I said.'

Dr Schneeweiss was too excited to argue. 'You mean, he's coming to Oxford? To All Souls?'

Dr Mottle began to show his impatience. 'Yes, that's exactly what I mean.'

Dr Schneeweiss clapped her hands together. 'I am most delighted to hear this, Dr Mottle. You have no idea how delighted. I'm familiar with *Portuguese Irregular Verbs*, which I would not hesitate – not for one second – to describe as the greatest work of Romance philology of our times. It's a real landmark in contemporary scholarship.'

Dr Mottle shrugged. He had no interest in Romance philology, and he was used to people who thought their particular discipline was the be-all and end-all. He had never met a professor who was not, to a greater or lesser degree, a *prima donna*, although he did accept that such people might exist. 'Sooner or later, everybody comes to Oxford.'

'Yes,' said Dr Schneeweiss, 'but what good fortune it is that Professor von Igelfeld is coming here when I am here. I am so pleased, Dr Mottle.'

Dr Mottle smiled. He liked to see the Visiting Fellows happy – life became so difficult when they became unhappy, as had proved to be the case with that professor from Harvard. Who would have known that that was going on? Who could have told?

He looked at his watch. He had a meeting to attend in a few minutes, but he would be free in the earlier part of that evening and he remembered that, although he liked to entertain every Visiting Fellow at least once to sherry in his rooms, he had not yet invited Dr Schneeweiss. He could kill two birds with one stone by inviting her this evening, along with this Professor von Igelfeld.

'I wonder,' he said to Dr Schneeweiss, 'whether you might care to join me for a glass of sherry this evening. Nothing formal – just a glass between six p.m. and seven p.m. sharp.' He knew that it sounded a bit strange to say 'seven p.m. sharp', but he knew from long and bitter experience that if he did not state a terminus he could be trapped for hours, particularly with somebody like Dr Schneeweiss, who had been reported to him as being exceptionally keen on long conversations.

Dr Schneeweiss accepted with alacrity. 'I have nothing on,' she said. 'It'll be a pleasure, Dr Mottle.'

'And I thought I might invite Professor von Igelfeld to join us,' Dr Mottle went on. 'That is, if he has arrived by then, which he assures me he will.' He paused. 'Have you ever known a German not to arrive when he says he's going to arrive, Dr Schneeweiss?'

She looked at him wide-eyed. 'Professor von Igelfeld?' she said.

'Yes,' said Dr Mottle. 'I thought I'd invite him too, unless, of course, you'd prefer for nobody else to be there.'

'Oh, no,' she reassured him quickly. 'I would be more than delighted to meet Professor von Igelfeld.'

'Good,' said Dr Mottle. 'And now, if you'll excuse me,

Dr Schneeweiss, I must attend a meeting.' He stopped. 'Actually, I might invite a couple of other visitors too. There are some Scottish people here for a conference, and I thought I might invite them. Professor Kenneth Reid and his wife, Professor Elspeth Reid.'

Dr Schneeweiss nodded. She did not mind who else was there; what mattered to her was that she was about to meet the world authority on Portuguese verbs. It did not matter to her who else was present at this Stanley and Livingstone moment. She would have sherry with the great Professor von Igelfeld and then invite him to dinner. They would go to the Randolph, which was comfortable and where they would be under no pressure to vacate the table for other diners.

She thought about von Igelfeld. At the moment, she assumed he knew nothing of her – not even that she existed. She hardly dared speculate as to whether he had read any of her papers; she thought it highly likely that he had not. Yet, after tonight, she would be a real person to him. She would be that American philologist with whom he had had dinner in the Randolph and whom he had then escorted back to her rooms at All Souls, and then invited to come to Regensburg and deliver, to a packed public audience, a resoundingly successful lecture on the attenuated subjunctive.

She would write to Notre Dame and tell them about it. She would send them a photograph of herself with Professor von Igelfeld. That would show them the company she kept, the impact she had. They might even regret – bless them, she

82

said to herself, for she was a kind person who liked to see the good in everybody – they might even regret not renewing her post-doctoral Fellowship. But I shall not be negative about Notre Dame, she thought, and especially now that I have Professor von Igelfeld.

sechs

Professor Plowson's Plot

Dr Mottle had invited Mrs Evans to stay on after work to help him entertain.

'I know it's a bit of an imposition,' he said to her. 'And I know that you have your husband to get home to.'

'No, no,' said Mrs Evans airily. 'This is one of Roger's fish nights – the Jericho Tropical Fish Society, you see. They meet and . . . and . . .' she ended lamely. They met and talked about fish, but she had difficulty in talking about it.

'That's very kind of you,' said Dr Mottle. 'You know these Visiting Fellows can be – hard work, by any standards. We don't have to worry about the Reids – they're no trouble – but this odd bird from Regensburg and poor friendly Dr Schneeweiss from Hicksville, Ohio . . . oh dear.'

'Notre Dame, Indiana,' she said. 'A nest of Romans, I believe.' She gave Dr Mottle a meaningful look and added, 'Just like Boston, with that tribe of Kennedys. Notre Dame is *teeming* with Opus Deites, I believe.'

Dr Mottle sighed. 'The Vatican has a great deal to answer for, hasn't it? The Inquisition, for one thing.'

'Unlike the dear old Church of England,' said Mrs Evans. 'We really set fire to so few people, and boiled virtually nobody in oil.'

'Some would say that the Church of England had no *conviction*,' said Dr Mottle. 'It takes conviction to do things like that to heretics.' He smiled. 'Do you think that the C. of E. might pick up a bit if it had the occasional show trial?'

'Possibly,' said Mrs Evans. 'It might help fill the pews. People are looking for something *vigorous*, you know.'

'Of course, we have our music,' observed Dr Mottle. 'People can always go to Evensong at the House.'

'Rome never were a match for us when it came to church music,' mused Mrs Evans. 'Morley, Bird and so on – none of them were R.C., were they?'

Dr Mottle thought of something. 'Do you think the Pope might take up a Visiting Fellowship here one day?'

Mrs Evans laughed. 'What a brilliant idea! A sort of ecumenical gesture, perhaps. It would be the beginning of the healing of a long split.'

'Just a couple of weeks. We could give him the Master's spare room and he could go and say his rosary each morning in the rose garden.'

They both laughed. 'Oh, we do have such fun,' said Dr Mottle.

They were interrupted by a knock on the door. 'Duty

calls,' said Dr Mottle, with a sigh. And then, 'I do wish these people would go away, but we must be hospitable, Mrs Evans, mustn't we?'

'We must,' she said. 'Even if it involves a certain measure of hypocrisy on our part.'

Dr Mottle, on his way to the door, stopped and turned to Mrs Evans. 'Have you ever thought of running away, Mrs Evans? I mean, just throwing in the towel and going off somewhere ... somewhere remote and away from all this. Costa Rica, for instance?'

Mrs Evans stared at him. Costa Rica. She opened her mouth to speak, but Dr Mottle had turned away and was now at the door. It was too late.

He opened the door to Dr Schneeweiss.

'I thought it might be you, Dr Schneeweiss,' he said. 'How delightful to see you.'

Dr Schneeweiss peered about the room. 'What lovely rooms,' she said. 'You are so lucky, Dr Mottle.'

Dr Mottle smiled graciously. 'I struggle to make the best of what is offered me,' he said. 'That, I think, is the duty of us all, whatever our station.'

'Sure,' said Dr Schneeweiss, squinting at a small framed print of an Oxford scene. 'And some places are better to struggle in than others.' She looked enquiringly at Mrs Evans. 'I haven't met your wife. I'm Andrea.'

Mrs Evans laughed, as did Dr Mottle. 'Secretary,' he said. 'This is Mrs Evans.'

There was another knock on the door. This time it was the Reids. They shook hands with Dr Schneeweiss and accepted a glass of sherry from Mrs Evans. The glass was very small, the sherry very dry. 'So dry, most of it has evaporated,' whispered Elspeth Reid to her husband.

Von Igelfeld was the next to arrive. The doorway was rather low for one of his height, and he had to incline his head as he entered the room. As a result, he did not see the reaction of Dr Schneeweiss to his arrival. She stood up straight, transfixed. She gripped the sherry glass she was holding so tightly that her knuckles turned white.

Dr Mottle brought von Igelfeld over to be introduced.

And Dr Schneeweiss fainted.

'My dear Dr Schneeweiss,' said Dr Mottle. 'The heat, I assume. These rooms get so uncomfortable in the heat.'

Dr Schneeweiss blinked. 'I guess I kind of fainted,' she said.

'You did,' said Mrs Evans. 'Would you like us to call a doctor?'

Dr Schneeweiss, who had been moved into an armchair by the combined efforts of Dr Mottle and the Professors Reid, now rose unsteadily to her feet. 'I'm just fine now,' she said. She looked about her, and saw von Igelfeld standing awkwardly, taking a sip of his sherry.

'Uncompleted introductions,' said Dr Mottle. 'Dr Schneeweiss, this is Professor von Igelfeld.'

Von Igelfeld bowed stiffly. 'I am so sorry that you fainted,' he said. 'But I am very relieved that you appear, now, to have recovered.'

Dr Schneeweiss moved over towards him. 'Oh, fainting's nothing,' she said. 'It's a bit like a power cut. Nothing unusual.' This was not strictly true; in fact, it was entirely false. Dr Schneeweiss could not remember the last time she had fainted – if she ever had; this was entirely the result of the extreme emotion involved in meeting von Igelfeld.

'Hah!' said von Igelfeld. 'A power cut! That is a very apt metaphor, I must say.'

The Reids now joined them. 'Professor von Igelfeld,' said Kenneth Reid. 'I believe that you're from Regensburg.'

Von Igelfeld bowed again. 'That is correct. I am in the Institute of Romance Philology there.' Soon, he thought, I shall be able to introduce myself as being the Director of the Institute of Romance Philology; but not just yet.

'We know somebody there,' said Elspeth Reid brightly. Turning to her husband, she asked, 'What is the name of that charming man we met in Paris – at the Sorbonne? He was giving a lecture there. He was from Regensburg, wasn't he?'

Kenneth nodded. 'Professor Unterholzer, I believe. Detlev Amadeus Unterholzer, I think was his full name.'

Von Igelfeld remained impassive, but internal questions came thick and fast. Charming? Unterholzer, with his plebeian nose and his loud laugh? Charming? What was Unterholzer doing in Paris delivering a lecture? Did the Sorbonne not know that there were scores of more suitable people to give lectures? Not only scores, but hundreds, in fact. Why had Unterholzer not mentioned going to Paris?

'We had dinner with him,' said Kenneth Reid. 'We went to a restaurant just off the Champ de Mars – a wonderful place. And then we went to the Opéra Bastille. I remember it so well. And Zimmermann was there with us too. Remember?'

Von Igelfeld struggled to contain himself. 'Zimmermann? Professor Zimmermann was there with you and . . . and . . .' The struggle was almost too much for him. 'With you and Unterholzer?'

Unaware of von Igelfeld's mental turmoil, Kenneth Reid confirmed Zimmermann's presence.

Von Igelfeld listened in dismay. 'Why was Professor Zimmermann there?' he asked. 'We do not see enough of him in general.'

'He was with Professor Unterholzer, I think,' said Elspeth Reid.

This was devastating news for von Igelfeld. That Unterholzer should have had the opportunity to have dinner at the same table as Zimmermann was bad enough – that he should have arrived at the restaurant *already in his company* was almost unbearable.

It was at this point that Dr Schneeweiss intervened. 'I must say, Professor von Igelfeld, that I am a very considerable admirer of *Portuguese Irregular Verbs*. In fact, I have brought a copy with me to Oxford.'

It was just what von Igelfeld needed to take his mind off

the painful picture of Unterholzer dining with Zimmermann in a restaurant off the Champ de Mars. Turning to Dr Schneeweiss, he smiled warmly. 'I am very pleased to hear that, Dr Schneeweiss.'

'It's a very fine book,' continued Dr Schneeweiss. 'Seminal.'

Von Igelfeld beamed with pleasure. Americans were difficult; he knew that there were many American academics in the field of linguistics who had no knowledge of *Portuguese Irregular Verbs*, and yet here was somebody who appreciated how very important it was. It was just the reassurance he needed after the shocking revelations about Unterholzer.

'It is some years since I wrote it,' said von Igelfeld. 'There are one or two places where I might amend it, if the opportunity were to arise.'

'I can't imagine much revision is required,' said Dr Schneeweiss. 'I think that everything that has subsequently been published has merely served to confirm what you first said in the book. You've been shown to be absolutely right.'

Von Igelfeld smiled as he took a sip of sherry. This was all very satisfactory. Earlier on that day he had felt some reservations about Oxford after he had been shown the room he was to have in All Souls, but this more than made up for that.

'I would be happy to discuss any aspects of *Portuguese Irregular Verbs* with you, dear Dr Schneeweiss,' he said. 'Indeed, it would be a privilege.'

Dr Schneeweiss's delight was palpable. 'Thank you,' she

said, reaching out to touch von Igelfeld lightly on the fore-arm in a gesture of gratitude.

Von Igelfeld decided to go further. 'Indeed, I wonder whether you would care to visit us in Regensburg.' He was thinking of the effect it might have on the others if an American so clearly entranced with *Portuguese Irregular Verbs* were to arrive at the Institute. It was all very well for Unterholzer to go off to Paris and have dinner with Zimmermann, but had he ever had so evidently star-struck an American enthuse over him? Von Igelfeld thought not.

Dr Schneeweiss swayed slightly, and for a few moments von Igelfeld thought she was going to faint again. He reached out to steady her, but she quickly recovered.

'I would love that,' she said quickly. 'I would just love that so, so much. I accept.'

Von Igelfeld was taken aback by the speed of her acceptance, but then he reminded himself of her enthusiastic remarks about *Portuguese Irregular Verbs*. It was only natural, he told himself, that she should be keen to come to Regensburg, and Americans, anyway, were not ones to delay things unduly. They acted quickly when the need arose; that was simply their way.

'When?' she asked.

Von Igelfeld shrugged. 'Whenever . . .'

She cut him short. 'When are you returning to Regensburg?' she asked.

'In three weeks' time,' he replied. 'This is a very short Visiting Fellowship I hold and . . .'

'That's fine,' she said. 'I'll come back with you.'

Von Igelfeld looked into his sherry glass. Had he been just a touch too encouraging? He had issued an invitation, though, and it must of course be honoured.

'That will be perfectly convenient,' he said.

'What are you doing for dinner?' asked Dr Schneeweiss. 'After this, I mean.'

Von Igelfeld looked at his watch. 'I am very tired,' he said. 'I was proposing not to have dinner.'

Dr Schneeweiss looked disappointed. 'What about breakfast?' she asked.

Von Igelfeld struggled. Was this the American way? Were they all like this? Very friendly and charming, but . . .

'I am not sure about breakfast,' he said quickly. 'I sometimes miss breakfast.'

'You have to eat some time,' said Dr Schneeweiss, playfully.

Von Igelfeld laughed nervously. 'Very funny,' he said. 'Yes, very amusing.'

sieben

HERMANN

Göttingen Calls

Life in the Institute was quieter now that von Igelfeld was away in Oxford. The sessions in the Senior Coffee Room were markedly diminished, as Prinzel had temporarily stopped attending them. He had done this before when von Igelfeld had been away, and the effect had always been the same: Unterholzer and Herr Huber were left to have coffee together. This led to a somewhat strained atmosphere, as Unterholzer tended to close his eyes while Herr Huber was speaking, and even on occasion had been known to snore while the Librarian was engaged in one of his longer stories about his aunt and the nursing home.

Herr Huber had suggested that, as a temporary expedient, Dr Schreiber-Ziegler might be invited to have her coffee with the two of them. 'There is more than enough coffee,' he said to Unterholzer. 'Now that Professor Prinzel is having his own coffee at his desk – as he is perfectly entitled to – not only is there more than enough coffee, but there are all these empty chairs. Would it not be more … more *friendly* to invite Dr Schreiber-Ziegler to join us? Only while Professor von Igelfeld is away, of course – it could be on the strict understanding that the privilege would be withdrawn once he returns.'

Unterholzer looked doubtful. 'It's a very radical suggestion, Herr Huber,' he said. 'I'm not sure that we should do something quite so dramatic as that.'

'But it would only be temporary,' urged Herr Huber.

Unterholzer shook his head. 'People don't distinguish between the temporary and the permanent as clearly as they should. In my experience, if you give somebody something, they think they have it for ever. It's human nature.' He paused. 'In fact, not only is it human nature, Herr Huber, it's canine nature too.'

Herr Huber listened attentively as Unterholzer told him about the family dachshund, Walter. 'Walter, as you know, was the victim of a veterinary accident and only has one leg.'

Herr Huber inclined his head sympathetically. 'I have heard about that, Professor Unterholzer. It was a very tragic matter, and I assure you that I have the utmost sympathy for …'

'Yes, yes, Herr Huber,' said Unterholzer impatiently. 'Your sympathy is very much appreciated. But the reason why I raise this is to illustrate the proposition that a benefit, once extended, is difficult to withdraw.'

Herr Huber took a sip of his coffee. 'I am sure you're right, Professor Unterholzer.'

'Yes,' said Unterholzer. 'I am. You see our sausage dog, Walter, has, as you know, a prosthetic appliance strapped to him – an undercarriage, so to speak, consisting of three small wheels. This means that he is able to propel himself along with his remaining leg. It works very well, except occasionally on hills, when there may be a problem.'

'There are no brakes?' asked Herr Huber.

'Precisely,' said Unterholzer. 'But that's not the point. The point is that Walter, like so many dogs, loves to get up on beds.'

Herr Huber chuckled. 'Oh, that's a very common thing with dogs, isn't it? My aunt – the one who's in the nursing home – I have two aunts, you know, Professor Unterholzer. One, you may already have heard me refer to, but then there's one in Berlin – she's my Aunt Trudi. She was married to a sea captain in Hamburg. They lived there for many years, and then they decided that when he retired they would go to live in Berlin because their daughter lived there. She's a teacher – not a fully qualified teacher, but one of those people who help in the classroom. She's actually hoping to get the teaching qualification at some point, but it's difficult for her to get enough time to study. And she's forty-eight now. She has a rather demanding boyfriend, you see – he's in his mid-fifties – who comes from Thuringia, from Erfurt, actually. I've nothing against Thuringia personally, Herr Professor, but you know what they're like over there. They can be a bit too conservative for my liking, frankly.'

Unterholzer, who had been studying his coffee cup carefully, pursed his lips.

'That aunt never had a dog,' Herr Huber continued. 'But my aunt – the nursing home aunt – she had a dog called Hermann. He was quite a fat dog, actually, and I used to call him Herr Göring, which my aunt did not think at all funny. And I suppose it wasn't, in retrospect, but there we are. Anyway, they gave Hermann a special treat once and served him steak for his dinner. It was a very bad mistake, because he wouldn't eat anything else after that. It had to be steak.'

'I see,' said Unterholzer.

'Yes,' said Herr Huber. 'They regretted it. Steak is such a price and you shouldn't really feed it to dogs.'

Unterholzer took a deep breath. 'The point I was going to make, Herr Huber,' he said, 'is not dissimilar. We allowed Walter to get up on to the bottom of our bed once when he was feeling a bit poorly. We made a little ramp for him, and he propelled himself up on that. But the next day he whined persistently until we put the ramp in position once again, and now he sleeps every night at the end of our bed. Frau Professor Dr Unterholzer – my wife – doesn't mind too much, but I would prefer not to have Walter there, especially if he moves from one side of the bed to the other and his wheels squeak. That can wake me up, you see.' He paused. 'So, the point is, Herr Huber, don't confer a benefit on anybody – on a sausage dog or a deputy librarian, it matters not – that you might need to withdraw. Expectations will be created.'

Herr Huber did not press the point, and no invitation was extended to Dr Schreiber-Ziegler. Coffee breaks continued, in their diminished way, marked by long monologues by Herr Huber, who seemed uncomfortable if there was silence. There were numerous bulletins from the nursing home, leavened with occasional accounts of the doings of neighbours. There were long expositions of a television serial Herr Huber and his wife were following, a rambling family saga set in Wiesbaden. There were detailed commentaries on the World Librarianship Congress that was to take place in Sydney the following year and that Herr Huber was possibly going to attend, his attendance being conditional upon his aunt's not taking a turn for the worse. 'Australia is very far away,' observed Herr Huber. 'Although if you actually live there, it isn't, is it?'

But then, three days after von Igelfeld's departure for Oxford, Herr Huber came into the Senior Coffee Room holding a page from the *DUZ Magazin*. He appeared excited and thrust the page eagerly into Unterholzer's hands.

'There is something here you need to read, Herr Unterholzer,' Herr Huber said. 'I have just seen it this morning.'

Unterholzer, who had been browsing the morning paper, sighed. Herr Huber was always finding items in journals and magazines that he imagined would be of interest to others, but which were usually not. He took the paper from the Librarian and adjusted his spectacles to read it.

'Here,' said Herr Huber, jabbing at the paper with a forefinger. 'This advertisement caught my eye, Professor Unterholzer – and you'll see why, I think.'

Unterholzer read with growing interest. The University of Göttingen was proposing to establish a new Chair, with its own new department, and were seeking applicants. The Chair would be in linguistics, with particular reference to historical aspects of the Romance languages. The holder of the Chair would be entitled to twelve assistants and generous grants for academic travel. There were no specified duties, other than to pursue research at the highest level.

Unterholzer looked up. 'This is very significant news,' he said.

'It's obviously a very prestigious Chair,' said Herr Huber. 'Only the very best appointments have no duties at all.'

'That certainly sounds very promising,' said Unterholzer.

'Do you think you might apply?' asked Herr Huber. 'Not that I, or anybody else, would want to lose you, of course.'

Unterholzer was uncertain. 'I'm not sure,' he said. 'I like the sound of this position, but Frau Professor Dr Unterholzer is very happy here in Regensburg.'

'But they say that Göttingen is a most agreeable town,' Herr Huber said. 'They have a very fine botanical garden there, with one of the most important collections of medicinal plants. Just think: your wife would like that.'

Unterholzer agreed that she would. 'I shall talk to her

about it, Herr Huber. I am most grateful to you for drawing the appointment to my attention.'

The following day, Unterholzer dropped in on the Librarian's office before coffee.

'I have given some thought to that matter you raised yesterday,' he began.

'The Chair in Göttingen?'

'Yes. I have spoken to Frau Professor Dr Unterholzer. She has been to Göttingen before, and likes it, but she is unwilling to leave Regensburg. As I told you, she is very happy here.'

Herr Huber nodded. 'I fully understand, Professor Unterholzer. And I must say, I am very relieved that you will not be going. Where would we – and, by that, I mean the whole Institute – where would we be without you?' He paused for a moment before answering his own question. 'I dread to think – I really dread to think.'

Unterholzer was touched by this compliment. It was rare for anybody to say anything nice to him, and even if this remark only came from Herr Huber, to whom nobody ever paid much attention, it cheered him to think that he meant something to the Librarian.

'You are very kind, Herr Huber,' he said, and then, in an act of supererogation – though prompted by Herr Huber's compliment – he enquired, 'And tell me, how is your aunt today?'

Unterholzer did not listen to the answer, which was every

bit as long-winded as he feared it would be. He was thinking about a possibility that had just occurred to him. Although a move to Göttingen would not be possible, he might still apply for the Chair. He would do this not with any intention of accepting the appointment if it were to be offered to him, but in order to be able to add an offer – if one were to be made – to his *curriculum vitae*.

Still feeling well disposed towards Herr Huber because of his earlier generous remark, Unterholzer decided to make the Librarian party to his plan. It was the right thing to do, he felt. It was Herr Huber, after all, who had drawn his attention to the position, and it would undoubtedly give him pleasure to know that something positive had come of his doing so.

'If I may tell you something in confidence, Herr Huber . . .' Unterholzer began.

Herr Huber nodded enthusiastically. 'Of course, Professor Unterholzer. Your confidences are entirely safe with me.'

Unterholzer lowered his voice. 'I think that I may apply to Göttingen after all.'

Herr Huber drew in his breath sharply. 'And leave Frau Professor Dr Unterholzer here in Regensburg?'

Unterholzer looked shocked. 'Certainly not, Herr Huber. No, I shall make the application and then, if they offer me the Chair, I shall turn it down.'

Herr Huber was puzzled. 'But why, Professor Unterholzer? What point would be served by that?'

Unterholzer smiled, and lowered his voice even further. 'Many people do that, Herr Huber. They apply for a Chair they have no intention of taking. Then they put it on their *curriculum vitae* that they turned down an offer from whichever university it is that offered it to them. That gives them additional status, and certainly it helps when they apply for a position that they really do want. Then people will say, *Oh, he was approached by such-and-such a university and turned them down – he must be in great demand.*'

Unterholzer brought his exposition to an end with a look of triumph. 'So, what do you think of that, Herr Huber?' he asked.

The Librarian hesitated for a few moments before replying. 'It's very cunning, Professor Unterholzer,' he said. 'It's very cunning indeed.'

'Thank you,' said Unterholzer. 'And it's all owing to you. You deserve the credit, Herr Huber. If you hadn't shown me that item in the *DUZ Magazin*, then it would not have occurred to me to apply.'

Herr Huber said nothing. He did not feel it was his place to criticise Unterholzer, but he deeply disapproved of what was proposed. Herr Huber was a Lutheran, and he believed very strongly in complete honesty, in all circumstances. He did not think it right to deceive the University of Göttingen in this way: they would expend time and energy on the processing of Unterholzer's application and, what was worse, his candidacy could mean that other serious contenders were denied a place on the short list. Unterholzer was bound to be a very serious prospect for the Chair, and that would probably preclude lesser applicants from finding their way on to the list of those called for interview. And then, once the offer had been turned down, the University would have to go to all the trouble of reconvening its appointments panel and conducting further interviews. Had Unterholzer not considered all that? he wondered.

'I hope your application meets with the success it so clearly merits,' said Herr Huber. And what it deserved, he thought, was no success at all.

'You're very kind, Herr Huber,' said Unterholzer. 'I'm sure it will.'

Château Phélan Ségur, 1961

Over the next few days von Igelfeld settled into the life of All Souls College. He spent much of his time in his room, or in the Codrington Library, working on a paper which he had done the groundwork for some time ago and only now had the opportunity to work on without interruption. He met Dr Schneeweiss for coffee on several occasions, but managed to fend off her invitations for lunch or dinner. She took his refusals in good stead, seeming to be happy enough to spend the odd hour or so in his company, bombarding him with questions about various passages in *Portuguese Irregular Verbs*. Von Igelfeld contained his impatience, and anyway he continued to be well disposed towards her, in spite of her importuning, on the grounds of her evident admiration for his work.

He had been in Oxford for a week when he received a note from Professor Plowson, inviting him to meet him for coffee in his room in the College.

'It's dreadfully remiss of me not to have been in touch before this,' the note said. 'I was assured by Mottle (poor chap) that you had been safely installed in your rooms, but I would still love to see you to find out if there is anything I can do to make your stay in Oxford a pleasant one.'

Von Igelfeld accepted the invitation to coffee, putting a note to this effect in Professor Plowson's pigeonhole in the Porter's box. The invitation was for the following day, and at the agreed hour von Igelfeld knocked loudly on the oak door on which a small wooden notice that said Professor Plowson might be found within.

Von Igelfeld had never met Professor Plowson, and so had no preconceptions as to what his host would look like. Even so, he was slightly taken aback when he found himself confronted with a man of astonishingly good looks – those of a ballroom dancing instructor, von Igelfeld thought: well groomed, his sleek, dark hair parted neatly down the middle.

'My dear Professor von Igelfeld,' said Plowson unctuously. 'What a particular pleasure it is to have you in the College with us.'

Von Igelfeld thanked him. 'The pleasure is mine too,' he said. 'The Codrington Library is a most congenial place to work, I must say.'

'Of course,' said Plowson. 'And you will have observed, no doubt, that it has a copy of your own great work *Portuguese Irregular Verbs*.'

It had been the first thing that von Igelfeld had checked up on when he had first used the Library. 'I am delighted that that is the case,' he said.

'Of course, I have found your book highly instructive,' said Plowson. 'There are so many inferior works of scholarship making it into print these days.'

'That is very worrying,' said von Igelfeld. He thought of Unterholzer's book on the subjunctive and Dr Martensen's book on the semiotics of Cistercian sign language.

'Thank heavens, I say, for the gold standard that certain major works give us,' continued Professor Plowson. 'And by that, of course, I mean works such as *Portuguese Irregular Verbs.*'

Von Igelfeld made a gesture of modesty. 'You are too kind, Professor Plowson.'

'But I mean it,' said Plowson. 'I assure you: every word is meant.'

Professor Plowson now poured a cup of coffee for his guest. 'There's something I wanted to raise with you, Professor von Igelfeld,' he said as he handed him the cup. 'It's delicate, but I feel this is the right time to raise it.'

Von Igelfeld waited.

Plowson put the tips of his fingers together, in the manner of a clergyman preparing to launch into prayer. 'What would your reaction be to receiving an honorary degree?'

Von Igelfeld took a moment to order his thoughts. He already had two honorary degrees, but they were both from

German universities, and the cachet of a foreign honorary doctorate was considerable – even irresistible.

'From Oxford?' he asked.

Professor Plowson inclined his head slightly. 'Yes, from this very University.'

Von Igelfeld smiled. 'I would be most honoured,' he said.

'That's marvellous,' said Professor Plowson. 'Of course, there are all sorts of hoops that we need to jump through before the degree is conferred, but I think I can assure you that with ...' and here he coughed modestly '... with my influence in high quarters, so to speak, we can be confident of the approval of the Hebdomadal Council, as we used to call it.'

Von Igelfeld bowed. He was already imagining the reaction of the Rector. That would show him a thing or two! Oxford! Let Herr Uber-Huber, with all his talk of elections and transparency, contemplate that.

'There is, however, one minor consideration,' Professor Plowson continued. 'In these matters there is often an element of – how shall I put it? – perceived reciprocity. My task in shepherding your nomination to a satisfactory conclusion would be considerably facilitated were your University, the University of Regensburg, to confer on some suitable person an honorary degree. Some suitable person from Oxford, that is.'

Von Igelfeld frowned. 'This would need to be done before the Oxford degree is conferred?'

Plowson nodded vigorously. 'That is exactly so,' he said. 'These matters are very delicate, but there can be no doubt but that the receipt by an Oxford recipient of a Regensburg honorary degree would mean that your own honorary degree would encounter very little opposition – indeed no opposition at all, I imagine.' He paused. 'I take it that there would be no difficulty in your arranging things at the Regensburg end? I imagine that someone of your international stature would encounter little difficulty with the University bureaucracy. Am I right in that assumption, Professor von Igelfeld?'

Von Igelfeld made a careless gesture. 'I don't think there would be any trouble.'

Plowson looked relieved. 'All that would need to be sorted out is the question of who – from the Oxford end of things – would be an appropriate recipient of the Regensburg degree.'

A silence ensued, to be broken eventually by Plowson, who sighed before he said, 'It might be simplest all round if I proposed myself. Not that I would wish to put myself forward, but purely to ensure the smooth passage of your Oxford degree, I might be prepared to receive a Regensburg degree.'

'You are very generous,' said von Igelfeld. 'I wouldn't wish to put you to any trouble.'

'It's no trouble at all,' said Plowson quickly. 'The important thing is to get your own honorary degree sorted out. And, to that purpose, I suggest you set the ball rolling at your end. We can provide you with all the necessary information about myself – for your committees and so on. I imagine you might want copies of my publications.'

'That would be helpful,' said von Igelfeld.

'And then,' Plowson continued, 'after Regensburg has conferred the degree on me, we can take the necessary steps here to confer ours on you.' He paused. 'I take it that's acceptable to you?'

Von Igelfeld thought for a moment. It was a pity that Plowson had to get his degree first, but he supposed that this was the way things worked. It did not particularly matter, though: the important thing was that he would end up with an honorary degree from Oxford. That was what counted more than any question of who went first.

Plowson refreshed von Igelfeld's coffee cup. 'Honorary degrees are rather odd things, aren't they? I'm pretty much indifferent to them myself, of course, but there are some people who would commit murder for one. Pretty odd. Of course, you have so many now, it's all the same to you, I imagine, but I did think, nonetheless, that it would be nice if Oxford joined the ranks of those who have honoured you.'

'I'm most honoured,' said von Igelfeld. 'And we at Regensburg are in turn most honoured that you will be enrolling as an honorary graduate of our institution.'

Professor Plowson beamed with pleasure. 'Contentment all round,' he said.

They parted on the best of terms. Professor Plowson said

that he looked forward to dining in college with von Igelfeld later that week. 'And, by the way,' he said. 'We should keep our little arrangement confidential for the time being. You know how envious people can get.'

Von Igelfeld agreed. Unterholzer was a prime example of that sort of academic envy and he could just imagine how badly he would take news of von Igelfeld's Oxford degree. Prinzel, by contrast, would take pleasure in his old friend's distinction. That was because he was secure, thought von Igelfeld. Prinzel had nothing to prove; Prinzel was confident in who he was and in his achievements. If others did well in something, his reaction was to congratulate them, not to feel threatened. Poor Unterholzer, thought von Igelfeld: his insecurity made it hard, if not impossible, for him to take pleasure in the success of others. It was really rather sad.

He left Professor Plowson's rooms and went out into the quad. It was now almost noon, and he thought that he might spend the hour before lunch in the Codrington, and then have a bowl of soup and a sandwich in the Fellows' Common Room before returning to his rooms to spend the afternoon working on his paper. As he crossed the quad, though, he became aware of a figure walking briskly towards him. As the other man approached him, von Igelfeld was able to make out that it was Professor Maclean, a scholar of the Renaissance and keeper of the College's wine cellar.

'My dear Professor von Igelfeld,' said Professor Maclean. 'I have been meaning to show you the College cellars.

Would you, by any chance, be free right now? I was just heading down there to check up on one or two things.'

Von Igelfeld hesitated. There were things that he wanted to do in the Codrington, but he did not want to be thought rude. He accepted the offer, and accompanied the genial Professor to the modest secluded entrance to the College's cellars.

'We have rather a lot of wine,' said Professor Maclean. 'Our cellars include substantial holdings of very old port. We sell a few bottles of that from time to time and invest in more day-to-day claret for the Fellows to have with their dinner.'

'Very wise,' said von Igelfeld.

Professor Maclean opened a gate that led further down into the cool foundations of the College buildings. Branching out on either side of a central corridor were large wine bins, most covered with a layer of dust. Aged bottles, laid down on stone shelves, receded into dim, half-lit corners.

'This is a very fine wine,' said Professor Maclean, gesturing to a row of bottles with faded labels. 'Château Phélan Ségur, 1961. Drinking exquisitely.'

'1961,' said von Igelfeld.

'Yes,' said Professor Maclean. 'Are you familiar with that vintage?'

Von Igelfeld nodded. 'There is a lot to be said for certain other years too,' he said.

'Oh, yes,' agreed Professor Maclean. 'But what other vintages would you have in mind?'

Von Igelfeld swallowed. 'I have a lot of time for 1993,' he said.

Professor Maclean raised an eyebrow. 'Really? I thought that was a very bad year. Those heavy rains in September and October . . .'

'I meant that 1993 was an interesting year,' said von Igelfeld. 'I didn't say it was a good year.'

'A thought-provoking distinction,' said Professor Maclean thoughtfully. He looked at his watch. 'Would you excuse me just for fifteen minutes or so? I have to go and check on something. Please browse around in my absence and when I come back we might treat ourselves to a little glass. We all have our personal supplies down here – mine are over there.'

He left von Igelfeld, who bent down to examine a cluster of ancient bottles. It was hard to make out the print on the faded labels. As he was peering at these, he noticed a movement behind one of the bins.

'Professor von Igelfeld?'

A figure stepped out of the shadows – a slender, dapper-looking man wearing a grey chalk-stripe suit and what looked like a College tie. 'Remarkable place, this,' he said in a clipped, polished accent. 'I sometimes come down here just to cool off. Air cooled by stone has such an agreeable smell, don't you think?'

'Yes, indeed,' said von Igelfeld. He was trying to remember where he had seen this man before. He was vaguely familiar – perhaps it had been at lunch in the College.

There were so many Fellows that it was difficult to know who was who.

'I should introduce myself,' said the man. 'My name is Blunt. I'm often referred to as B.'

'B?'

'Yes, B. But Blunt will do. I really don't mind Some people call me nothing at all.'

'I see.'

Blunt now gestured in the direction of the darker reaches of the cellar. 'Shall we go and take a look at some of the College port?' he asked.

Without waiting for an answer, Blunt gently led von Igelfeld by the elbow down the narrow corridor between the wine bins. As his voice lowered, he said, 'This College, of course, is fertile ground for recruitment. Our side, you see, has to make sure that we maintain our assets. There's always a bit of attrition. The weaker brethren fall by the wayside. Chaps cross over. Chaps disappear for one reason or another – lose conviction, give up – there are any number of reasons why one would want to get off the active list.'

Von Igelfeld said nothing. He had no idea where this strange conversation was leading. But in a way he was not surprised: nothing was as it seemed in this University; nothing made sense in quite the same way it made sense in Germany.

Blunt stopped and pointed to a row of ancient bottles, largely obscured by dust and cobwebs. 'Frightfully good port, that stuff,' he said. 'Lovely nutty taste. Goodness knows how old. Wasted on the Portuguese, of course, but they very wisely send it over here.' He paused. 'We would be very discreet, you know. You can count on us for discretion.'

Von Igelfeld was at a complete loss. 'I'm very sorry, Mr Blunt . . . '

'Oh, do call me B,' said Blunt.

'B, I'm sorry, but I don't understand.'

Blunt laughed. 'Very convincing,' he said. 'Some of the other side are irretrievably literal. They don't get irony – not in the slightest.'

'No?'

'No. Not at all. But to get back to where we were, so to speak, we'd regard you as a sleeper. We'll call on you at some point – and we really do feel that you have the ideal cover, being the author of that book – what's it called again?'

'*Portuguese Irregular Verbs.*'

'Yes, that's the one. Marvellous – quite marvellous. Nobody would suspect that the chap who wrote that mouthful – that stuff – could be working for us. Perfect.' Blunt reached into a pocket and withdrew a card. 'This is me. You can ring that number any time of the day or night. Any time at all. Ask for B, but, if I'm not available, try J and O. Poor O – she gets some very rum phone calls, but there we are. But in the meantime don't do anything – just wait. We'll be in touch.' Blunt looked at his watch. 'Heavens! Is that the time? I must be on my way. Frightfully good talking to you, and I'm glad we're on the same page. HMG very much appreciates this, you know, Professor von Igelfeld.' He paused. 'Shall we call you V? For von? Would that be acceptable?'

He slipped back into the shadows, leaving von Igelfeld on his own. He had no idea what had just happened, but he was not sure that he approved of it. Who was HMG? Why did they appreciate what he was said to have done, when he had done nothing at all? And why had B chosen him of all people for whatever it was that he claimed to be doing?

There were many unanswered questions, and Oxford was beginning to confuse him, with its opaque rituals and its curious eccentricities. I shall go back to Germany, he said to himself. Germany was rational; Germany was comprehensible. Oxford, All Souls, England – these were all mysteries whose real meaning was elusive – a will-o'-the-wisp, an *ignis fatuus*, on the surface of a fast-moving stream; a cloud whose shape changed as you beheld it; a parallel universe existing in a vale of allusions and ambiguities.

neun

Unterholzer: Shocking
News Emerges

It was Herr Huber who welcomed von Igelfeld back to the Institute.

'It doesn't seem like three weeks,' the Librarian said. 'And yet in other respects it does. Not having you here, dear Professor von Igelfeld, has meant that we have been counting the days to your return.'

Von Igelfeld acknowledged the compliment with a nod. Then he asked, 'All of you? All of you have been counting the days?'

Herr Huber looked uncomfortable. 'I speak for myself, of course.' He recovered. 'But yes, I'm sure that the others were too. Professor Dr Dr Prinzel, for instance ...'

'And Professor Dr Unterholzer?'

Herr Huber's embarrassment returned. 'Professor Dr Unterholzer ... Yes, of course.' He lowered his voice.

'Actually, Professor von Igelfeld, Professor Dr Unterholzer has been a bit preoccupied over the last few days.'

Von Igelfeld enquired why.

'You know about his dachshund, Walter?'

It was von Igelfeld's turn to feel awkward. Walter was permanently on his conscience, as it was he, von Igelfeld, who had been indirectly responsible for the dog's misfortune. There had also been the incident when von Igelfeld had tripped over him at a dinner party at the Unterholzers' and had sought – with limited success – to oil the dog's wheels with olive oil.

'I'm aware of the dog in question,' muttered von Igelfeld.

'Well,' continued Herr Huber, 'poor Professor Unterholzer has been very exercised over an incident that took place near his house. He was taking Walter for a walk – as he does every morning – and he was stopped by a policeman. By two policemen, in fact. They were very abrupt with Professor Unterholzer – presumably they did not realise that they were dealing with a full professor. You know how the police can be sometimes, Professor von Igelfeld. One of the nurses at my aunt's nursing home – a male nurse – was treated very badly by the police the other day. He told me that he had been to a bar with his girlfriend and the police were looking for somebody in connection with a drugs matter. He is definitely not involved in drugs – as you can imagine a male nurse will know the risks of that sort of thing . . . And what, we might ask, are the police doing going into bars?'

Von Igelfeld interrupted him. 'Yes, Herr Huber, that is all

undoubtedly true. But what happened on this walk? Why did the police apprehend Professor Unterholzer?'

Herr Huber looked pained. 'It is very unfair, Professor von Igelfeld. The police are taking a very narrow view – very narrow indeed.'

'Of what, Herr Huber?'

'Of the situation, Herr Professor.'

Von Igelfeld sighed. 'Of what situation, Herr Huber? What situation are they taking a narrow view of?'

Herr Huber looked about him, as a police informant might do before passing on information. 'Professor Unterholzer's offence. I think they are being very ... how shall I put it? Very pedantic, perhaps. Or *strict*. Yes, I think the right word is *strict*.'

Von Igelfeld drew in his breath. Now he, too, lowered his voice. 'Are you telling me, Herr Huber, that Professor Dr Unterholzer is being *prosecuted* for an offence?'

Herr Huber nodded miserably. 'I believe that to be the case, Professor von Igelfeld.'

It took von Igelfeld a full minute to recover. 'This is shocking,' he said at last. 'This is profoundly shocking, Herr Huber.'

'Indeed it is. Try as I might, I cannot remember any incident in the history of the Institute that even approaches this situation.' He paused. 'There was, of course, that occasion when Dr Schreiber-Ziegler came into the Coffee Room. But no, although that was a shock, it was not in quite the same league as this.'

Von Igelfeld was struggling with conflicting emotions. He was genuinely shocked that Unterholzer was facing a criminal charge, and he felt a natural sympathy for his colleague, but, at the same time, Unterholzer had been asking for this sort of thing for years. Sooner or later, if you lived by the sword, you died by the sword. And then there was simple curiosity. What on earth had Unterholzer done? Could it be something truly scandalous – an offence of the sort that ended up being reported at length in *Das Bild* or the equivalent? There were so many cases in which respectable people were suddenly revealed to have done something apparently out of character, and these cases of course attracted a lot of attention. A particular form of *Schadenfreude* came into play here: people loved to see the high cast low. And what better character for such a public morality play of that nature than a professor of Romance philology *and* an author of a major work (well, major only because there was not much competition) on the imperfect subjunctive?

The Librarian now revealed the nature of Unterholzer's offence.

'Professor Unterholzer was taking Walter for his morning walk, you see,' Herr Huber began. 'They were walking along the pavement that runs down his street – you know, the pedestrian part – and a police car pulled in and out got two policemen. They informed Professor Dr Unterholzer that he was committing an offence by a using a vehicle on the pedestrian section of the road.'

Von Igelfeld frowned. 'But you said he was walking.'

'Professor Dr Unterholzer was walking, but the police, you see, said that his dog, having wheels, *was considered a vehicle*. Therefore, he was using a vehicle on a pedestrian-only pathway.'

For a few moments, von Igelfeld could not think of what to say. Herr Huber was right – that seemed to be a very narrow, technical interpretation of the law. And yet, and yet ... If the police started to interpret the law in a broad fashion, then they would have far too much discretion in its enforcement. And that, thought von Igelfeld, could lead to uncertainty in the law, which was precisely what one wanted to avoid. That was why there was a *Strafgesetzbuch* – a Criminal Code – in the first place.

At last, von Igelfeld spoke. 'I'm very sorry to hear all this, Herr Huber. And I much regret the adverse publicity that this will very obviously bring to the Institute.'

Herr Huber agreed. 'I have already heard from Herr Uber-Huber about it,' he said. 'He had read an item in the newspaper reporting the charging of Professor Dr Unterholzer. He said this is precisely the sort of thing that His Magnificence the Rector wishes to avoid.'

'And quite rightly so,' said von Igelfeld.

Herr Huber made a gesture of resignation. 'We shall just have to bear it,' he said. 'The law will have to take its course.'

'You know what would happen if this occurred in Japan?' von Igelfeld asked.

Herr Huber shook his head. 'They are very sensitive to shame, I believe.'

'Yes,' said von Igelfeld. 'So if this happened in Japan, Professor Dr Unterholzer would commit *hara-kiri*. With a sword. That is undoubtedly what would happen.' He remembered something. 'You may recall, Herr Huber, what happened to that poor Japanese professor who visited the Institute a few years ago. He was called Professor Akitoshi Nishimoto. He was an acknowledged expert in Japanese word endings.'

'I remember Professor Nishimoto quite well,' said Herr Huber. 'He was a very courteous man, as they all are. He was very surprised to discover that the Institute was not made of paper. He always bowed when he arrived in the morning and I bowed back and so he bowed again, and I never knew how to stop the series of bows. Sometimes it lasted for ten minutes or so.'

'Well, he tried to commit *hara-kiri*,' said von Igelfeld, 'after his theory of word endings was shown to be wrong in some minor particular. But apparently the sword he used was blunt, and so he merely scratched his stomach rather badly. He resigned from the editorial board of the *Japanese Philological Quarterly* as a result. It was all very sad. Of course, the editorial board of the *Japanese Philological Quarterly* had quite a turnover, as they were always committing *hara-kiri* for one reason or another. I believe they kept a sword in the cupboard of the editorial offices for that very purpose.'

'I don't think Professor Dr Unterholzer will try to commit *hara-kiri*,' said Herr Huber.

'No, possibly not,' mused von Igelfeld. 'But we shall

have to watch him closely, I think. It will be a very difficult time for him.'

Von Igelfeld had not been accompanied by Dr Schneeweiss on his journey back from Oxford, in spite of her suggestion that they should travel together. This would not be possible, he said, as he had the proofs of a forthcoming paper to correct and would need to do that on the ferry journey. So she agreed to arrive two days after his return. 'I am *so* looking forward to spending time in the Institute,' she enthused. 'I feel I already know it – and the colleagues there. Detlev Amadeus, for example, and Florianus, of course.'

Von Igelfeld had been unable to conceal his shock at her use of first names. 'I'm terribly sorry to point this out to you, Dr Schneeweiss, but the use of first names is severely restricted in Germany. I take it that you were referring there to Professor Dr Unterholzer and Professor Dr Dr Prinzel. We would *never* use their first names.'

Dr Schneeweiss looked surprised. 'But why not? If that's what they're called . . .'

'Their mothers may call them that,' interjected von Igelfeld. 'And a few very old friends. But we *never* use first names in the Institute.'

'But why not, Moritz-Maria?'

This was almost too much for von Igelfeld. For a few moments he struggled with the temptation to rescind Dr Schneeweiss's invitation, but then he reminded himself of the kind things she had said about *Portuguese Irregular Verbs*. She was a fan of his work – a true fan – and the least he could do was to put up with her bizarre American notions.

'I think it might be best if you continued to call me Professor von Igelfeld, Dr Schneeweiss. I would never wish to be considered formal, but that is how I'm used to being addressed.'

'If that's what you want, that's fine by me,' she said. 'When in Rome, and all that.'

'When in Regensburg,' quipped von Igelfeld, and laughed loudly at the joke. That helped to defuse the tension and they had parted with an agreement that they would meet in Regensburg. In the meantime, von Igelfeld would send a message to Herr Huber asking for a library user's card to be made out in the name of Dr Schneeweiss, and for an arrangement to be made to find a desk for her.

He had also asked Herr Huber to speak to Dr Schreiber-Ziegler about taking Dr Schneeweiss under her wing. 'Dr Schneeweiss is a most charming person,' he had written, 'but she has a very enquiring mind and enjoys asking questions. I am sure that she and Dr Schreiber-Ziegler will get on very well and will share many interests.'

With his usual willingness to help, Herr Huber had gone out of his way to ensure that Dr Schneeweiss's requirements were met. Accommodation had been arranged for her in a small flat owned by the University and made available to

Institute visitors. In the Institute itself, a desk had been placed in an alcove at the back of the Library, and Herr Huber had filled the drawers with stationery, a map and guidebook to Regensburg, a book of bus tickets, and a small folding umbrella. When she had arrived, he had given her a personal tour of the Institute – excluding the Senior Coffee Room, which he had merely pointed to with the cursory explanation that this was a room set aside for the private use of long-term staff of a certain seniority.

'Not for me, then,' said Dr Schneeweiss, laughing.

Herr Huber had also laughed, but only out of politeness, and quickly moved on to show her where she might hang her coat and, if she chose to use a bicycle, where she might park it securely. Over coffee, taken in his office, he had told her about his aunt and the nursing home and the incident with the faulty fire sprinkler. Dr Schneeweiss had listened with interest and said that she would love to meet Herr Huber's aunt – if a visit could be arranged. Herr Huber had replied that it certainly could, and his aunt would love to hear about America, which she had never visited but said that she hoped to see one day. 'That, of course, will never happen,' said Herr Huber.

'You never know, Herr Huber,' said Dr Schneeweiss. 'Look at me: I never imagined I would meet Professor von Igelfeld, but then I did. And now we're working together. Just think about that.' She glowed with pleasure. 'You see, you should never give up, should you?'

'I suppose you're right,' said Herr Huber. Had he given

up? He rather thought that he had, but perhaps there was a chance for him to do great things. Such as? Move the Library's comparative linguistics material to a new position? Go to yoga lessons in India – at an ashram?

'Perhaps I could even show your aunt around Pittsburgh – if she made it to the States.'

Herr Huber smiled. 'She'd love that. She'd love Pittsburgh.'

'Or New York,' Dr Schneeweiss continued. 'I could show her New York.'

Herr Huber imagined his aunt at the top of the Empire State Building, and he would be standing beside her, pointing out the sights. And she would say, 'And which way is Germany?' And he would point to the east, over the blue smudge of the ocean, and his aunt would make one of her usual observations about how, when people are having lunch in one part of the world, in another they're having breakfast. And all New York would be beneath their feet.

zehn

For Vulgar Readers

Before he went into the Senior Coffee Room that morning, von Igelfeld took a deep breath. He had made a point of not going in early, so that he would not find himself alone with Unterholzer – if Unterholzer were to be the first to arrive. That would be potentially very awkward, even if Unterholzer were to assume that von Igelfeld did not know the shocking news of his arrest and imminent prosecution. Von Igelfeld wondered what etiquette required one to say when meeting a friend or colleague charged with a criminal offence: did one express regret, or sympathy, perhaps? Or did one say nothing about what surely would be something of an elephant in the room – and in that case studiously avoid any reference to any matters pertaining to the police, or crime, or even justice in the broadest sense? The problem with being a member of a respectable segment of society was that you knew nothing of correct form in such circumstances, because you would rarely encounter anybody who was in trouble with the police. It would be different, von Igelfeld imagined, down amongst those who had a disregard for the law and for whom an arrest, or even a spell in prison, was perfectly socially acceptable.

To von Igelfeld's relief, not only was Prinzel there with Unterholzer when he entered, but also Herr Huber. The Librarian was regaling the company with a long story about a letter that had been incorrectly addressed and had been opened in error by the Matron of his aunt's nursing home.

'The letter was a very vulgar one,' he said. 'It was from a man who was writing to a lady in very frank terms about a recent trip they had made together. Matron read it all the way through and was outraged that anybody could write such things and then consign them to the German post.'

Unterholzer laughed. 'Why did she read to the end?' he asked. 'Surely it would have been obvious at the very beginning of the letter that it was intended for somebody else.'

'I believe she thought it her duty,' said Herr Huber. 'She felt that she needed to know the sort of thing that was going on.'

'Oh, there's a lot going on all right,' said Prinzel. 'I've always known that the students, for example, are up to something of that sort.'

'You see them whispering to one another,' said Herr Huber.

Von Igelfeld's arrival brought this conversation to a close.

'Ah!' exclaimed Prinzel. 'The wanderer returns.'

'Returned from Oxford,' said Unterholzer.

Von Igelfeld acknowledged the welcome. 'It is very good to be back,' he said. 'England is a very strange country.'

'Indeed, it is,' said Prinzel. 'And it is inhabited by very peculiar people: you never know if they mean what they're saying.'

'Or if they mean anything at all,' added Unterholzer. 'Which explains the irrationalities of the English language.'

Von Igelfeld agreed. 'The regularity of a nation's verbs is a measure of the rationality of a culture,' he pronounced. 'English is full of quirks, and that should be a warning signal of the nature of the people.' He paused, but not for so long that he might lose their attention. 'And what has been happening in my absence?'

This question might have been innocent enough in any other context, but it was fraught with peril in that particular place at that particular time.

Herr Huber cleared his throat. 'What has been happening?' he said quickly. 'Well, at my aunt's nursing home there has been a major issue with the arrest of one of the cooks . . .' He stopped as he realised that he had inadvertently wandered straight into the very area that his sudden intervention was intended to avoid.

Prinzel adopted a pained expression. 'We have had some very heavy rain,' he remarked.

Von Igelfeld looked at Unterholzer, who averted his eyes. Prinzel looked at Herr Huber, who looked at the floor. After

Prinzel's remark on rain, nobody said anything for a few minutes. In his nervousness, Herr Huber slurped his coffee noisily, causing the level of his own embarrassment to rise yet further.

Von Igelfeld experienced a certain satisfaction in all this. Unterholzer could hardly complain; he had plotted against the established order in the Institute for years now, hoping to replace von Igelfeld as the academic leader – if not the actual director – of the Institute. Now that plan lay in ruins because of his having run foul of the local police. What could he expect? No, he must face the consequences of his reckless behaviour, and, if these included awkward moments in the Senior Coffee Room, then so be it.

Von Igelfeld decided to end the silence with a final observation on the situation. 'Of course,' he began, his tone deliberately casual, 'one doesn't really want *too much* to happen, does one? There is a balance between having extreme events on the one hand and *stasis* on the other. Neither is desirable, I think.' He paused, and took a sip of his coffee. 'But, be that as it may, let's not dwell on such questions; let us move on to more positive matters. You will have seen that I have returned with a young ... how should I put this? ... a young *fan* of my work, Dr Schneeweiss, an American.'

Prinzel smiled. 'A follower, Herr von Igelfeld? You are very fortunate. Normally it's only rock stars who have *followers*.'

'Professor von Igelfeld said *fan*,' Herr Huber corrected.

'And I have met this fan of yours, Herr Professor, as you know. I hope that she is happily settled in.'

Von Igelfeld thanked him. 'I'm most grateful, Herr Huber. She seems to be getting on very well. She'll only be here for a couple of months, I believe – indeed hope – but in that time I imagine that she will get a lot of valuable work done. She's an expert on the subjunctive, as I think you may know.'

This brought a sharp reaction from Unterholzer. *He* was the expert on the subjunctive, and it was intolerable that von Igelfeld should go around picking up – for that was what it amounted to – *unauthorised* experts on the subjunctive, just because they expressed a – misguided – enthusiasm for his work.

'I'm surprised that you didn't consult me about this . . . this young girl,' Unterholzer said gruffly.

'Oh, she is not a young girl,' pointed out Herr Huber. 'She is a lady in her late twenties, I would say. She is very attractive, if I may venture to say.'

Von Igelfeld's eyes narrowed. 'Yes,' he said. 'Herr Huber is, as usual, quite right. Perhaps, Herr Unterholzer, you were too preoccupied with *other matters* to pay much attention to our visitor.'

'Oh!' said Prinzel. This was an involuntary expression of surprise. Von Igelfeld was getting perilously close to spelling out Unterholzer's embarrassment, and that, Prinzel thought, was uncalled for.

Unterholzer sensed that too, and decided to fight back. 'I may not be in a position to notice everything that's going on, Herr von Igelfeld, but that's probably because my head is not very readily turned – unlike the heads of some, perhaps, which can be turned by younger women who profess to have read their work.' He paused, and took a meaningful sip of coffee. 'Not that I am thinking of any particular instances of such a phenomenon; and not that I suspect many young women actually read the sort of thing that draws them to *older men* and to the flattery of these *older men* – if you see what I mean.'

Herr Huber, ever helpful, ever the mediator, the averter of conflict, said, 'My aunt has a friend, you know, who married a much younger man. She was forty-five at the time, and she met this young man of eighteen who came to deliver a parcel to her house. It was a hot day, and she invited him in. He never properly left the house, I understand, and a month later they were married. My aunt was shocked. She said that no eighteen-year-old will know his mind – especially in a situation like that where there is a woman of that age and experience waiting to pounce on him.'

Unterholzer laughed. '*Pounce*, Herr Huber? Do you think she actually *pounced*? Perhaps she hid behind a door and then leaped out on to the young man. Perhaps that is what happened.'

'They call such women *cougars*,' observed Prinzel. 'I read about them in the paper.'

'In the *Frankfurter Allgemeine Zeitung*?' asked von Igelfeld. 'I don't think I saw anything about that.'

'There are more vulgar papers,' said Unterholzer. 'These papers like to write about these matters. Their vulgar readers are very interested in such things.'

'Such as the reports of what goes on in criminal courts,' muttered von Igelfeld, glancing at Unterholzer as he spoke, and then quickly looking away.

Unterholzer said nothing. Then Herr Huber intervened once again. 'I do not see why they call them that,' he said. 'A cougar is a sort of lion, is it not? What is the similarity between these ladies and lions?'

'They prowl,' said Prinzel, with a degree of relish. 'Perhaps this Dr Schneeweiss, who has accompanied Herr von Igelfeld back to Germany, was *prowling*.'

'Oh, I do not think so,' said Herr Huber. 'I have spoken to her. She is a particularly agreeable young woman, with a serious interest in Romance philology. She has even expressed an interest in visiting my aunt's nursing home in order to meet her.' He paused: an unlikely thought had occurred. 'Imagine if I took a lioness to the nursing home. Imagine if I led her into my aunt's room and said, *Aunt, I've brought you a visitor*. And the lioness sauntered through the door and jumped on to the bed, perhaps. Imagine that!'

They all stared at Herr Huber, who looked down into his coffee cup.

'I don't think we should be too fanciful in our

conversation,' said von Igelfeld. 'The world is in a parlous enough state, what with the rising crime rate ...'

Less than an hour later, as von Igelfeld was sitting in his office, attending to the mail that had piled up in his absence – at least four letters – a knock at his door preceded the hesitant appearance of Herr Huber.

'I don't want to disturb you, Professor von Igelfeld,' the Librarian began. 'I know how much you have to do.'

Von Igelfeld looked up from his correspondence. 'I am very busy, Herr Huber,' he said. 'As you no doubt can see. All these letters ...' He gestured to the mail in front of him.

'I can just imagine it,' said Herr Huber. 'That is why I hesitate, but I feel that I should raise something with you.'

Von Igelfeld sighed. 'Well, Herr Huber, please do, although ...' he glanced at his watch '... time is short, as you know.'

Herr Huber edged into the room. 'Professor von Igelfeld,' he began, wringing his hands as he spoke, 'this is most embarrassing for me. I know that I am just the Librarian and that it is not for me to tell the academic staff what to do.'

Von Igelfeld nodded. 'That is undoubtedly the case, Herr Huber. You are a librarian. Librarians have many important duties – I would be the first to acknowledge that – the very first. However, those duties do not include telling academic staff anything ... Or indeed telling *anyone* anything.'

Herr Huber plucked up his courage: it was not easy to talk in this register to the author of *Portuguese Irregular Verbs*. And yet there were times when duty required that one speak out as a citizen rather than as a librarian. This, he thought, was one such time. 'Quite so, Professor von Igelfeld. And yet ...' He swallowed hard. 'And yet I must say that I was a bit taken aback by your tone with poor Professor Dr Unterholzer. It is a very difficult time for him.'

Von Igelfeld bristled. 'A difficult time, Herr Huber? If it's a difficult time, then it is a difficult time of his own creation. Perhaps he should have thought of the consequences before he flagrantly breached the terms of the law.'

'Yes, but ... but you may not be aware of what Professor Dr Unterholzer is proposing to do.'

Von Igelfeld waited. Then he said, 'How can I tell what he's proposing to do, Herr Huber? I'm not a mind-reader, for heaven's sake.'

'No, no, of course you're not, Professor von Igelfeld. But you see, Professor Dr Unterholzer has been planning to make a major gesture in your direction. In view of your imminent elevation to the post of Director, he has been planning to vacate his office in your favour.'

This was a bombshell. By a quirk of the room allocation system, Unterholzer had for the last few years occupied the largest office in the Institute. Von Igelfeld had often reflected on the injustice of Unterholzer's having the office he did, but had not been able to do anything about it. Now here was Unterholzer apparently preparing to correct this anomaly by spontaneously offering the office to him, presumably in exchange for his own office.

'I'm at a loss for words,' stammered von Igelfeld. 'I really am . . .'

Herr Huber smiled. He was emboldened now. 'It is a very noble gesture on Professor Dr Unterholzer's part. And that is why I felt that your attitude at coffee this morning might have been a bit . . . a bit out of place. Not that I would dream of criticising you, or indeed anyone else, Professor von Igelfeld.'

Von Igelfeld shook his head. 'No, Herr Huber, you are quite right to raise that with me. Even though you are only a librarian, had you gone further and censured me, it would have been nothing but well deserved.' He paused. He felt appalled at having made the remarks he had to Unterholzer when all the time Unterholzer was planning this remarkable act of selfless generosity. 'I am very sorry that I was less than charitable to him this morning. Who amongst us can cast the first stone, Herr Huber?'

Herr Huber seemed relieved. 'I am very glad that you understand, Professor von Igelfeld.'

'Of course I understand, Herr Huber,' said von Igelfeld. 'And I am most grateful to you for drawing my attention to my thoughtlessness. I shall remedy this immediately by seeking out Professor Dr Unterholzer and making a full apology.'

Herr Huber breathed a sigh of relief. 'That would be much appreciated, I think.'

'And do you think,' continued von Igelfeld, 'that he will make the offer of his room at this point? Shall I raise it with him?'

Herr Huber was confident of what would happen. 'I think that he will bring it up himself.'

'He is a remarkable man,' said von Igelfeld. 'We are fortunate indeed to be able to count him as a colleague.'

Herr Huber agreed. 'We are indeed.' And now it was perhaps time to speak from the heart. 'I remind myself every day, Professor von Igelfeld – every single day – of how fortunate we are to have this Institute, with these colleagues, and with these resources to change the world. We are so lucky.'

Von Igelfeld rose to his feet. 'I shall go immediately,' he said. Then he added, 'How soon do you think, Herr Huber, shall I be able to move into my new office?'

'Professor Dr Unterholzer implied that this could be done more or less straight away,' said Herr Huber. 'He has already spoken to Herr Wagenknecht – one of the University porters – about having his books moved. Herr Wagenknecht is standing by. So perhaps tomorrow?'

Von Igelfeld smiled with pleasure. 'That would be acceptable. In fact, more than acceptable – it would be most satisfactory.'

'It's a very fine office,' said the Librarian. 'In fact, it's worthy even of His Magnificence the Rector.'

Von Igelfeld made a dismissive gesture. 'He would hardly appreciate it. I doubt if a man like that requires many bookshelves.'

He ushered Herr Huber out of his room and made his way to Unterholzer's office, rehearsing his apology on the way. 'Look here, Herr Unterholzer,' he might say. 'I know you're in trouble with the law, but I shouldn't have alluded to that. I'm very sorry, and I hope you will forgive me.' And Unterholzer, he hoped, would say, 'No harm done, Herr von Igelfeld, and I was wondering whether you might care to exchange rooms with me, now that you are our Director-elect, or soon to be elect.'

Which was more or less what happened, with the result that the following day von Igelfeld found himself newly ensconced in Unterholzer's considerably more spacious office, while the helpful Herr Wagenknecht took Unterholzer's books off the bookshelves and placed them on a trolley for wheeling down the corridor to von Igelfeld's old room.

And that was where he was sitting when Herr Huber appeared again and said, 'I don't like to disturb you in your new room, Professor von Igelfeld, but there is a troublesome matter I need to discuss with you.'

Von Igelfeld gestured towards a chair. 'Don't concern yourself, Herr Huber. When I am Director, I shall be available at all times – at all times – for any member of staff who has troublesome issues to air.'

'It's about Professor Dr Unterholzer,' said the Librarian.

'Ah,' said von Igelfeld. 'After coffee, perhaps.'

Herr Uber-Huber and Non-elitism

Herr Uber-Huber stood in the corridor outside Professor Dr Dr Prinzel's office, his right knuckle poised to knock on the door. His was an officious presence in every respect: a dark suit embraced his slightly corpulent figure, a carefully knotted tie graced the front of his shirt, and a small, discreet gold-plated badge, a symbol of some obscure civic organisation, caught the light from the ceiling lamp, flashing it back as a warning signal. In his left hand he clutched a file, a bureaucrat's shield against the slings and arrows of academic recalcitrance.

On responding to Prinzel's called-out *Kommen Sie herein*, the University official found Prinzel at his desk, an open copy of an Albanian dictionary in front of him. On looking up and seeing Herr Uber-Huber, Prinzel tapped a page of the dictionary and remarked, 'Very interesting, Herr

Uber-Huber. I've discovered that Albanian has something it calls *pastërma*, which is defined as dried meat. That sounds remarkably like *pastrami* or the Romanian *pästramä*. The Romanians – or some of them – are always looking for Latin roots in their loan-words – they hate to allow anything that isn't traceable to a Latin origin.'

Herr Uber-Huber muttered, 'Typical!' but left it at that.

'But I mustn't burden you with such matters,' said Prinzel, closing the dictionary. 'You have a university to run, and that's no simple matter, is it, Herr Uber-Huber?'

Herr Uber-Huber was not sure how to take this. It was possible that Prinzel was doing no more than referring to the complexity of university administration, or it could be a veiled and resentful reference to the intervention of the central university administration in the affairs of the Institute. Either interpretation was possible, but he would, for the time being, assume that Prinzel was merely being polite.

'As you know,' Herr Uber-Huber began, 'His Magnificence the Rector is taking a close interest in the proposed governance reforms of your Institute. He – that is, His Magnificence – and I have spent not a little time, Herr Prinzel, in devising what we think is a modern, transparent, non-elitist and progressive structure for the smooth running of the Institute.'

Prinzel waited. This was the *prolegomenon*. The important part was to follow.

'I have here,' Herr Uber-Huber continued, 'the results of our labours. It must be brought to the attention of those who work in the Institute, even if you have, as we recently discovered, no Director.' He looked reproachfully at Prinzel. 'In normal circumstances, a document of this nature would be forwarded to an Institute Director, but in this case ...' There was a further reproachful look.

Prinzel tapped the Albanian dictionary in a way that conveyed his fading patience. 'I'm looking forward to hearing your proposals, Herr Uber-Huber – in fact, we all are.'

'Not proposals,' said Herr Uber-Huber quickly. 'Rules. The Rector has enacted the scheme for the governance of the Institute. The word *proposals* suggests an inchoate regime. That is not the case. The Institute now has a scheme of governance that is fixed and implemented.'

'I see,' said Prinzel, through gritted teeth.

Herr Uber-Huber sat down, uninvited. That was presumably part of the new rules, thought Prinzel grimly: university bureaucrats may sit down wherever, and whenever they like, without being invited to do so by the professors of the Institute.

Extracting a sheet of paper from his file, Herr Uber-Huber slid it across the desk to Prinzel. 'This is the new set of rules, Herr Prinzel. You will see the Rector's signature at the foot of the page, which signifies the official status of the procedures.'

Prinzel ran his eye down the page. 'It's a very untidy

signature, Herr Uber-Huber,' he said. 'In fact, how can one tell that this document has been signed by the Rector, when all it has is a ridiculous scribble at the foot of it?'

The bureaucrat looked at Prinzel through narrowed eyes. 'I would not refer to the Rector's signature in those terms, Herr Prinzel,' he warned.

Prinzel raised an eyebrow. 'Herr Uber-Huber, I would remind you that I am a full professor of this University. Under the terms of Article 65 of the *Bayerisches Hochschulgesetz*, I can only be removed by an act of the State Parliament. I do not believe that similar protection is afforded to ordinary officials of the University. Correct me if I'm wrong, but that is my understanding of the situation.'

The retort struck home, and Herr Uber-Huber made a conciliatory gesture. 'I was not intending to give offence, Herr Prinzel,' he said. 'I suggest that you take a quick look at the new rules so that I can elucidate anything that requires elucidation.'

Prinzel looked at the sheet of paper. As he read, his expression became one of increasing concern. Herr Uber-Huber, noticing this, smiled.

'Is there anything worrying you?' he asked unctuously.

'Am I to understand that this list of persons here will all – *all* of them – be entitled to vote for the new Director?' asked Prinzel.

Herr Uber-Huber nodded. 'Yes. The policy of the University is to be non-elitist – as you know. We therefore decided – or, rather, His Magnificence decided – that those entitled to vote would be all three full professors – yourselves, in fact – plus the Librarian Herr Huber, and the Deputy Librarian Dr Schreiber-Ziegler. In addition, we – I mean the Rector – determined that there should be an external person allowed to vote. This is standard procedure, as you know, in Chair appointments. We get somebody who is not a member of the University – an outsider – to ensure fair play, so to speak.'

'Yes, but—'

Herr Uber-Huber cut Prinzel off. 'In this case, it seemed to us that it would be simplest – and least expensive – to use an outside scholar who is currently visiting, and so we cast about and realised that you have an American scholar visiting at present, a Dr . . .' He consulted his papers. 'A certain Dr Schneeweiss. She, you will note, is a person of the female persuasion.'

Prinzel's mouth had opened, and was stuck there.

'And then,' Herr Uber-Huber went on, 'we were keen to include a representative of under-represented classes. We considered all of you and I'm afraid we reached the conclusion that none of you has particularly convincing credentials in that respect, and so we have included Frau Schlaginhauffen of the University canteen, as a further eligible voter. Frau Schlaginhauffen, you will recall, occasionally arranges the catering for the Institute when you hold events. She is known for her expertise in serving

Müncher Weisswurst and so she is what we call a legitimate stakeholder. I further believe that she is on good terms with Dr Schreiber-Ziegler, as is Frau Pommelsbrunn, the cleaner. She will be entitled to a vote as well.'

Prinzel took a deep breath. 'Are you mad, Herr Uber-Huber? Is the Rector mad? Do you – does he – have the slightest idea of what Romance philology is?'

Herr Uber-Huber bristled. 'Excuse me, Herr Prinzel, but calling other people mad is not a very non-elitist thing to do. In fact, it is anything but.'

'Oh really,' exploded Prinzel. 'This is just too much. I never thought I would see the day when a German academic institution would be offered on a plate to those who have no academic qualification in the discipline in question – all in the name of non-elitism.'

'Well, you are now seeing that day, Herr Prinzel,' said Herr Uber-Huber, rising to his feet. 'So get over it, perhaps.'

Prinzel rose to his feet too. 'One moment, Herr Uber-Huber. One moment. How non-elitist are you, may I ask?'

'Non-elitist? What do you mean?'

'Well, you are a man,' said Prinzel. 'And men are often elitist. What is more, you are quite a fat man, if I may say so, Herr Uber-Huber, which suggests prosperity, doesn't it? You are dressed in an expensive suit, and, what is more, you call yourself *Uber-Huber,* in order to distinguish yourself from the ordinary, common-or-garden Hubers. Is that non-elitist? Is that progressive? I don't think so, Herr Gross Uber-Huber, or Herr Hoch Uber-Huber or whatever. I don't think so at all.'

Herr Uber-Huber spun on his feet. 'I didn't come here to be insulted, Herr Prinzel. And you may be sure that the Rector will hear what you said about his signature. I shall write him a memo to that effect the moment I get back to my office. I shall lay it all before him. I shall tell him exactly what you said about his signature being a ridiculous scribble.'

'Phooey,' said Prinzel.

'What?' shouted Herr Uber-Huber.

'Phooey, Herr Huber Squared. *Zweimal* phooey!'

At coffee that morning, Prinzel tapped the table and asked for silence. The others – von Igelfeld, Unterholzer, and Herr Huber – all looked at him expectantly; they had all noticed that he seemed to be in a state of shock, and now they hoped to hear the reason why.

'I have devastating news to report,' Prinzel began. 'I received a visit this morning from Herr Uber-Huber.'

Von Igelfeld frowned and looked thoughtfully into his coffee cup. Unterholzer sighed.

'He has given me the rules for our directorial election,' Prinzel went on. 'And I am afraid to say that we shall be outvoted. It's as simple as that. We shall be outvoted.'

Nobody said a word. Prinzel went on to explain about

the expanded franchise. He said that it could be assumed that Dr Schreiber-Ziegler would control the votes of her three friends: Dr Schneeweiss, Frau Schlaginhauffen the *Müncher Weisswurst* lady, and Frau Pommelsbrunn the cleaner. 'That gives her a bloc of four votes, including her own. So if she herself stands, and votes for herself – which she certainly will do – she will be the new Director. *A deputy librarian will be Director.*' He glanced at Herr Huber. 'Your *junior*, Herr Huber. Your *junior* colleague will have authority over you. You might care to consider the implications of that.'

Unterholzer frowned. 'Excuse me, Herr Prinzel, but I'm not sure that you're right. There may be four of them, but if I'm not mistaken there are four of us: myself, Professor Dr Dr von Igelfeld, yourself, and our dear Herr Huber. That's four.'

'So, it'll be a draw,' said von Igelfeld.

Prinzel sighed. 'Only for a short time. The rules state that in the event of a draw the Rector may intervene with a casting vote, and we all know in which direction his vote would be cast.'

'Dr Schreiber-Ziegler?' asked Unterholzer.

'Yes, he's made it very apparent he favours her.'

'We're finished,' announced von Igelfeld. Suddenly it seemed to him that nothing counted for anything any longer. *Portuguese Irregular Verbs*, the honorary doctorates, the editorship of the *Zeitschrift*, the conferences in Rome,

Palermo, Lyons – none of that counted for anything. It was all meaningless.

Prinzel looked up. 'We are *not* finished, Herr von Igelfeld. I have a plan.'

'It's too late,' muttered Unterholzer. 'We have been outmanoeuvred.'

Prinzel shook an admonitory finger. 'No, we haven't. Just listen.'

He told them of his plan. At the end, once he had finished, von Igelfeld looked at Unterholzer. 'Well, Herr Unterholzer, what do you think of that?'

'It might work,' Unterholzer replied, adding, 'On the other hand, it might not.'

'We shall see,' said von Igelfeld. 'I think it might work because we have right on our side.'

Both Unterholzer and Prinzel agreed that this was a powerful factor in their favour. They certainly had right on their side, because Dr Schreiber-Ziegler and her legions were radical revolutionaries, determined to destroy rather than to build up. They deserved to lose, and, if there were any justice in the world, that was what would happen. But Justice, for all her strengths, may sometimes require a bit of a helping hand, and that was where Prinzel's plan came into it.

Herr Huber looked uncomfortable. 'This plan of yours, Professor Prinzel,' he said hesitantly. 'Do you think it's a morally acceptable one?'

Prinzel grinned. 'You have to fight fire with fire, Herr Huber,' he said.

Von Igelfeld agreed. 'Herr Prinzel is right, Herr Huber. We must play these people at their own game.'

They left the Senior Coffee Room and returned to their offices. They were more cheerful now, as it would not be long before they would be fighting back. That made them feel less helpless in the face of the machinations of Dr Schreiber-Ziegler and her like. We may be surrounded, thought von Igelfeld, but perhaps we are not finished after all. This encouraging thought made him break out into a hum, just under his breath. It was Wagner, and it seemed just right for the moment. For his part, Prinzel broke out into a few *sotto voce* bars of Orff's *Carmina Burana*, but did so in the wrong key and he soon gave up. Unterholzer, who was tone-deaf, remained silent, but allowed himself a slight smile of satisfaction. These people would be shown what was what in due course, and everything would return to normal, or what passed for normal. Really – why did people try to change things that did not need changing? Why could people not just mind their own business and not go round looking for people to torment with their new notions and all their busybody intervention? These people would find out the error of their ways in due course and he, Detlev Amadeus Unterholzer, would be magnanimous in victory. You had to be. There was no point in being petty in this life. You had to adopt a broad canvas. You had to show generosity. You had to do all of that, while at the same time you preserved the good things that needed preserving. One of these was the Institute, and its current way of doing things. That *had* to be protected. It had to be, and Prinzel's brilliant idea would do just that.

zwölf

Caribbean Creole

Later that morning, having knocked timidly at the door, Herr Huber was admitted to the new office in which von Igelfeld was still busy installing himself.

'I am very pleased with my new office,' said von Igelfeld as Herr Huber crossed the room to approach his desk. 'There is so much space: far too much for poor Professor Dr Unterholzer, with his rather meagre collection of books, but just right for me, I must say.'

Herr Huber looked around. His librarian's eye noticed that von Igelfeld's arrangement of his books did not follow the Institute's recommended order, but this was not the time, he thought, to raise the matter.

'It's a very spacious room,' said von Igelfeld. 'It was so generous of Professor Dr Unterholzer to exchange rooms with me – a truly noble gesture.' He paused. 'It is always encouraging, is it not, Herr Huber, to encounter altruism in this world? There are so many selfish people who think entirely of themselves.'

The Librarian agreed. 'I am very much opposed to selfishness,' he said. 'There is a woman at my aunt's nursing home who eats all the strawberry jam on the table – every scrap of it – before the others get a look in. My aunt has spoken about this on several occasions.'

'Shocking,' said von Igelfeld.

'And then there is the question of hot water,' continued Herr Huber. 'Over the past couple of years my wife and I have been going for our holidays in Austria. There is a hotel near Klagenfurt that we like. It has very good views of the Wörthersee, but it does not have a good hot water system. There is never enough.'

Von Igelfeld shuffled a sheaf of papers on his desk. The Librarian's stories could go on and on, meandering according to a logic – or lack of logic – of their own. Here we were in Klagenfurt, for instance, and hot water was the subject . . .

'We always seem to go there at the same time as a man from Cologne – a very stout man who goes there with his girlfriend, who paints her toenails bright red. Very bright red, in fact – you can't miss them when she wears her sandals . . .'

'Yes, yes, Herr Huber. That must be most distracting, but . . .'

'He – this man from Cologne – he gets up early for a bath each morning and uses all the hot water – all of it. My wife thinks that he lies in the bath and keeps the tap running, allowing the water to drain out of the overflow pipe – you know those pipes they have at the top of the bath so that the bath won't overflow. Do you know those pipes, Professor von Igelfeld?'

'Yes, I do, Herr Huber, but let us not spend too much time thinking about them.' He glanced at his watch. 'My goodness, look at the time. I will have to get on with things or I shall have spent my entire morning achieving nothing.'

Herr Huber cleared his throat. 'I was hoping to speak to you, Professor von Igelfeld. I was hoping to have a word with you about Professor Dr Unterholzer.'

Von Igelfeld looked up. 'Ah, Professor Dr Unterholzer. Yes. I suppose we should give some thought to his predicament. Do you think he might get a prison sentence? It would be a bit extreme, I think, for what is, after all, a relatively minor offence, but the authorities might wish to make an example of him. That's possible, I suppose.'

'Oh, I don't think they would send him to prison,' said Herr Huber. 'The offence in question really is very minor – operating a vehicle on a pedestrian track is hardly—'

'Don't be so sure,' said von Igelfeld. 'It could be argued that taking a vehicle on to the pedestrian pavement is really dangerous. You could harm somebody, you know. That's why that particular law exists, I should imagine.'

'Yes, but the vehicle in this case was a dog,' pointed out Herr Huber. 'I grant you that it was a dog with wheels, but it was rather different from, say, a car or a motorcycle. Those could be a threat to pedestrians, but not a dog.'

'Possibly,' von Igelfeld conceded.

'But that isn't really what I wanted to talk about,' said Herr Huber. 'There is another very difficult matter connected with Professor Dr Unterholzer. It has been weighing on my mind. It has even stopped me sleeping.'

Von Igelfeld raised an eyebrow. What on earth had Unterholzer got up to now? Was he perhaps wanted by Interpol for money-laundering, or something of that nature? Stranger things had happened, although one would have to admit that that would be very strange indeed.

'I felt this morning that I just had to unburden myself,' said Herr Huber. 'I could not in conscience countenance what Professor Dr Unterholzer is proposing to do – or, I think, has already done.'

Herr Huber now had von Igelfeld's complete attention. 'You're quite right to speak about this, Herr Huber. A problem shared is a problem halved. That's what they say, isn't it?'

Herr Huber closed his eyes. His expression was pained as he told the story of Unterholzer's application for the Chair in Göttingen. Von Igelfeld listened, and when Herr Huber had finished, he was wide-eyed.

'So he has no intention of taking up the Chair, should it be offered to him?'

'That is the case,' Herr Huber confirmed. 'It's all a ploy.'

Von Igelfeld shook his head. 'I had heard that this sort

170

of thing goes on,' he said. 'I heard that Professor Burggrub does this from time to time. Indeed, I heard that sometimes he even applies for Chairs that are not in his field at all. He applied for a Chair of Chemistry in Stuttgart, I'm told, although he's a professor of Medieval History. He said in his application that he did not know a great deal about chemistry but was very strong on departmental administration and on *spreadsheets*, whatever they may be. I'm told they were furious. They wrote to him and said that they thought his application disrespectful and they were surprised that he had nothing better to do.'

This triggered an observation from Herr Huber. 'I had an uncle who was a chemist,' he said. 'He knew nothing about medieval history, of course—'

Von Igelfeld cut him off. 'Yes, yes, Herr Huber, quite so, but let us concentrate on Professor Dr Unterholzer and his . . . well, I have to use the word – his dastardly scheme.'

Herr Huber lowered his gaze. 'I feel awkward talking about it,' he confessed. 'I feel that I'm betraying a confidence, but I don't think we can let him get away with this. We owe it to the University of Göttingen to do something.'

'I completely agree,' said von Igelfeld. 'Should we write to them and warn them? Is that what you're proposing to do?'

Herr Huber was quick to claim otherwise. 'No, Professor von Igelfeld. I was thinking of something different. I was thinking that you might apply for the Chair.'

Von Igelfeld shook his head vigorously. 'Out of the question,' he said. 'What would happen to this place if I left? No, impossible, Herr Huber.'

'But you wouldn't leave,' said Herr Huber. 'If you applied for the Chair, that would knock Professor Dr Unterholzer out of the running. They would never consider him above you.'

Von Igelfeld made a modest gesture. Herr Huber was quite right, of course. 'But then, Herr Huber? What then?'

'In your application, you would ask them not to consider any other Regensburg candidates, as you would not like word to get out that everyone wanted to leave Regensburg. They would understand that, I think, and would do as we wished – because they would be so pleased to be getting you. So they would then make a list of candidates for interview that would have you on it – at the top, I imagine – with one or two others from other universities. Berlin, perhaps. Or Hamburg maybe.'

'And Professor Dr Unterholzer?'

'They would write to him saying that he was not on the short-list. Then, once that has happened, you would withdraw, saying you had changed your mind, and they would then interview the others on the short-list and give the Chair to one of them.'

'But might they not come back to Professor Dr Unterholzer and make his application active once more?'

Herr Huber said that he thought this unlikely. 'They

would lose face that way, I think. I feel sure that they would opt for one of the short-listed candidates.'

Von Igelfeld looked at the Librarian with new admiration. 'That is a very clever plan, Herr Huber – I'm quite surprised.'

Herr Huber thanked him. 'So, you'll do it?'

'With pleasure,' said von Igelfeld. 'I wouldn't want you to fret, Herr Huber: we all rely on you, you know.'

'You are very kind, Professor von Igelfeld,' said Herr Huber.

That afternoon, von Igelfeld made his way to the Institute's Library. He was working on a paper for a conference on Creole languages, and had reached an exciting point in his investigations of Portuguese influences on Papiamentu, a language spoken on the Caribbean islands of Curaçao, Aruba and Bonaire. There was a claim that Papiamentu was an offshoot of an earlier Portuguese-based pidgin, but this theory had been doubted by those who detected greater Spanish influences. A great deal was at stake in this debate, and passions had been raised. Von Igelfeld knew that he had to tread carefully, and that the world – or part of it at least – would be waiting for his conclusions with bated breath.

Von Igelfeld was leaving no stone unturned in his research. He had located a copy of Rodolfo Lenz's seminal study, *El Papiamento, la lengua criolla de Curazao: la gramática más sencilla,* reprinted from the 1926 volume of the *Anales de la Universidad de Chile,* and was paging through this when he became aware of Dr Schneeweiss at his side, peering over his shoulder.

'Papiamentu,' she said. 'How interesting, Moritz-Maria.'

Von Igelfeld shuddered at the use of his first name, but he bit his tongue. He was aware that they were but days from the election of the Director, and Dr Schneeweiss was, after all, one of the electorate.

'This is Lenz's study,' he said 'It is the first port of call, I think. One of the earliest, if not *the* earliest, account of the language.'

Dr Schneeweiss nodded. 'Yes, I know that.' She rested a hand lightly on his shoulder. The effrontery of it, thought von Igelfeld. The sheer effrontery. Is that what they did in America? Paw one another in libraries?

'I did field work out there,' Dr Schneeweiss continued. 'Not for long – just three months – when I was working on my Ph.D. at Columbia. I learned to speak it – not very well, but a bit.'

Von Igelfeld could not conceal his surprise. 'You? You learned Papiamentu?'

Dr Schneeweiss smiled. 'Would you like me to tell you a story – or begin a story – in Papiamentu?' She did not wait for him to answer. '*História di un máma ku jú.* Story of a mother and a son. *Un día taba tín un mama ku su jú, i nan taba ta masa póber.* One day there was a mother and her son and they were very poor. *E tata taba ta piskado* ... The father was a fisherman ...'

In spite of his irritation at being disturbed, at being addressed by his first name, and at having Dr Schneeweiss's hand on his shoulder, von Igelfeld had to admire this display of knowledge of such an obscure language. 'I am most impressed, Dr Schneeweiss,' he said.

Dr Schneeweiss basked in the compliment. 'Perhaps I could work with you on your paper,' she said.

Von Igelfeld pursed his lips. Really, this was quite beyond what was acceptable. A junior author *never* invited himself or herself to assist in a paper: the invitation *always* had to come from the senior researcher.

'Perhaps,' he said, purely out of politeness.

'Good,' said Dr Schneeweiss. 'When shall we start?'

Von Igelfeld stared at the text of Professor Lenz's article. 'I'm not sure,' he said. 'I hadn't planned ...'

Dr Schneeweiss cut him short. 'I believe I can get hold of Silva-Fuenzalida's *Papiamentu Morphology*,' she said. 'It's a North Western dissertation, but I know somebody who has the text on his computer.'

Von Igelfeld sighed. 'That would be very useful,' he said. And it would, and he wished he could be more enthusiastic, but Dr Schneeweiss was just impossible. He looked at her, and she smiled down at him.

It now occurred to him that he might use this moment of rapport to raise the issue of the election.

'Dr Schneeweiss,' he began. 'I imagine that Dr Schreiber-Ziegler has told you about our impending election and about how the Rector is keen for you to act as the external assessor.'

Dr Schneeweiss nodded. 'Yes, she has. And I'm quite happy to do it – especially if the Rector wants me to.'

'He does, I believe,' said von Igelfeld. He paused. 'I'm not sure if you are aware of this, but I myself will be standing for that post.'

Dr Schneeweiss frowned. 'But I heard from Dr Schreiber-Ziegler that she's hoping to be Director. She's already asked me to vote for her.'

Von Igelfeld caught his breath. He should not have been surprised by that, but it was still a shock to hear the news spelled out.

'And will you vote for her?' he asked, and then added, 'And why?'

'She said that it was time there was a woman Director,' said Dr Schneeweiss. 'And I can see the reasoning behind that. Women need to have their fair share of these posts, you know.'

'Of course they do,' said von Igelfeld. 'But only, surely, if they are qualified for the post. Dr Schreiber-Ziegler has many talents, but she is not a philologist. This is an institute of Romance philology. It follows, then, that it should not be run by a librarian. Librarians may run libraries – I would never seek to do that myself – but institutes should be run by professors.'

'Why are there no women professors in the Institute?'

asked Dr Schneeweiss. 'I don't wish to sound rude, but shouldn't there be some female professors?'

The question completely floored von Igelfeld. 'Because . . .' he began. And then stopped. 'You see . . .' he resumed, but then stopped again.

Dr Schneeweiss removed her hand from his shoulder. 'I'm sure it'll all turn out for the best,' she said. 'Whichever way it goes, life will go on.'

She returned to her desk at the back of the Library, leaving von Igelfeld staring at the open volume before him. He was still staring at it half an hour later, having turned not a single page, and wondering how it was that everything was turning out so badly. Perhaps he should go to Göttingen after all. How many assistants were being offered to the new holder of the Chair there? Twelve? It was very tempting.

He went back to his office just before four in the afternoon. The mail had arrived, and he noticed that there was a letter from Oxford. He wondered whether this was from Plowson, giving further details of the proposed honorary degree. But it was not. It was from Blunt, the man he had met in the wine cellars of All Souls, who had made some utterly opaque remarks about his joining something or other at the instance of HMG, whoever that obscure personage might be.

My dear V,

I do hope that your return to Germany went well. I myself have just been in Warsaw for a few days. I'm now back in Oxford, where we are enjoying a very nice spell of settled weather. I do a bit of Morris dancing, as I may have mentioned to you, and my side has been practising quite hard for a dance meeting we're having at Blenheim next week. We're up against some strong competition.

I was slightly surprised by some of the developments that occurred while I was in Warsaw. You'll remember Professor Plowson, I take it. Well, the poor fellow is in hospital and likely to remain there for several weeks yet. Apparently, somebody – some prankster – had stuck a sign on his back saying Kick Me. Some juvenile undergraduates saw this and gave him a kick, sending him tumbling down a set of stairs. They ran off, as one would expect them to, and nobody knows who put the sign there in the first place. Anyway, I went to see Plowson in hospital; he's not very popular round here, I'm afraid, and I believe that I was the only visitor he had received in the Radcliffe apart from a fire-eater from a circus that has been camped outside town for a few weeks now. Very odd, that, but there we are.

The other news from All Souls is that Dr Mottle, whom you will remember, has disappeared. There's a theory that he's gone off to Costa Rica, but you know how these rumours are usually baseless. By an extraordinary co-incidence, his secretary has disappeared too. These things happen in threes, of course, and so we're all standing by for the next bombshell!

I'll be in Germany in the autumn, and so I thought I might look you up. Keep your eyes peeled eastwards, and give me a call the moment you see anything that strikes you as significant – unusual troop movements, that sort of thing. As I mentioned to you, you can always get me on that number I gave you, but you can also get J and O if I'm away from my desk. They'll know exactly who you are and can act quickly, if necessary.

Sincerely, my dear V,

B.

dreizehn

Transparency *Redivivus*

Two days later, at eleven o'clock in the morning, the time when they normally met for coffee, Professor Dr Dr Moritz-Maria von Igelfeld, Professor Dr Dr Florianus Prinzel, Professor Dr Detlev Amadeus Unterholzer and Herr Huber congregated in the Senior Coffee Room and listened intently as Prinzel explained what was to happen.

'I have scrutinised the rules as delivered to me by Herr Uber-Huber,' Prinzel announced. 'They require that we post a notice stating the time of the election. They do not say where the notice has to be posted, nor how far in advance of the proposed election.'

'Are you sure about that?' asked Unterholzer. 'Normally these things require advance warning to be given. Normally you'd expect . . .'

Prinzel cut him short. 'I have read and then re-read the rules, Herr Unterholzer. If we put up a notice now, there is nothing to stop us from holding the election this afternoon at two o'clock.'

Von Igelfeld was concerned about the notification of Frau Schlaginhauffen and Frau Pommelsbrunn, neither of whom was in the building at the time. 'What about those two ladies?' he asked. 'A notice posted in the Institute would hardly constitute proper warning.'

'That is admittedly true,' Prinzel conceded. 'And, for that reason, I telephoned both of them this very morning. Both of them have been informed.'

'And are they intending to vote?' asked von Igelfeld.

Prinzel nodded. 'They both said they would be here at two and would cast their votes. I told them that voting papers would be available in the Senior Coffee Room.'

'That seems to me to be entirely fair and above board,' said Unterholzer. 'I would not wish to disenfranchise either of those two ladies – even if they are likely to vote for . . .'

'Dr Schreiber-Ziegler,' supplied von Igelfeld.

Prinzel, reluctantly, with the air of one acknowledging the inevitable, inclined his head. 'I imagine that is what they will do,' he said. 'Or, shall I say, that is what Dr Schreiber-Ziegler will have instructed them to do.'

'So your plan,' said Unterholzer, 'depends for its success on Dr Schreiber-Ziegler and Dr Schneeweiss not seeing the notice and therefore being unaware of the need to vote.'

'Yes,' said Prinzel. 'The notice will say that voting must be done between two and three in the afternoon. That is often a time when Dr Schreiber-Ziegler is engaged in cataloguing. She buries herself in her work – I've seen her do it. She won't see the notice.'

'And Dr Schneeweiss?' asked Unterholzer.

Prinzel looked at von Igelfeld. 'That is where you come in, Herr von Igelfeld. You will distract her. She is always very keen to hear what you have to say about anything. Send her off on some errand in the Library – finding something or other. Checking a complicated reference perhaps.' He paused. 'Then, at three o'clock, the voting will be over. We shall examine the ballots and discover that there are four votes for you, Herr von Igelfeld, and two votes for Dr Schreiber-Ziegler. Those will be the votes cast by Frau Schlaginhauffen and Frau Pommelsbrunn.'

There was a silence as they each reflected on their role in the plan. Then Herr Huber asked, 'Where will you post the notice of the election, Professor Prinzel?'

'In the men's washroom?' suggested Unterholzer, and laughed.

Herr Huber looked scandalised. 'That would be most improper,' he said. 'I could never countenance such a thing.'

'Relax, Herr Huber,' said Unterholzer. 'That was only a joke.'

'This is no joking matter,' sniffed Herr Huber.

They drank their coffee in silence. At one point, Herr Huber started to report on the latest affairs of his aunt's nursing home – some story about a missed delivery of vitamin supplements – but he soon realised that nobody was listening, and the story trailed off. Silence returned.

At one-thirty, Prinzel put up the notice advising of the election. This was placed on the Institute's main noticeboard in the entrance hall, a prominent enough place, but only likely to be seen by those entering the Institute and *not by those already in the building*. He then photographed the noticeboard in order to prove, if called upon, that the notice had been duly posted.

'My camera prints the time and date on the image,' he said to von Igelfeld, who watched him do this. 'We shall have firm proof if they try to say there was no notice.'

Von Igelfeld said nothing, as did Herr Huber, who was also watching. After Prinzel had gone back to his office, Herr Huber drew von Igelfeld aside.

'Professor von Igelfeld,' he whispered, 'I cannot be party to this. I have tried to go along with Professor Dr Dr Prinzel's plan, but I'm afraid I simply cannot countenance it.' He paused, and looked reproachfully at von Igelfeld. 'And you, Professor von Igelfeld: I never thought that you, a gentleman, a nobleman even, would allow yourself to be drawn into such a plan.'

Von Igelfeld looked at the Librarian. Here was Herr Huber, a man of very ordinary background, drawing his attention to what honour required. He was right. He was absolutely right, and he, von Igelfeld, should hang his head in shame that he had even contemplated being part of an underhand trick of this nature. And directed against women, too. He closed his eyes. Oh, the shame. What would his grandfather say were he to witness this conduct on the part of a von Igelfeld? What would any of his forebears think were they to see him stooping so low as to deceive Dr Schreiber-Ziegler and Dr Schneeweiss in this way?

Von Igelfeld drew in his breath. 'Herr Huber,' he said, 'you and I must go into the Library and inform Dr Schneeweiss of the time of the election. Then we must seek out Dr Schreiber-Ziegler in her office and draw her attention to the imminent vote.'

Herr Huber's relief showed. 'I knew that you would say that, Professor von Igelfeld. I knew that as a man of honour you would decline to follow Professor Dr Dr Prinzel's shabby lead.'

Von Igelfeld defended Prinzel. 'He is doing it with the best of motives, Herr Huber. Herr Prinzel is trying to save the Institute from disaster. We must not be too harsh on him.'

'I know that,' said Herr Huber. 'But it is still wrong, and I am glad that we are doing what we are doing.'

Prinzel froze when he saw Dr Schreiber-Ziegler and Dr Schneeweiss present themselves at the Senior Coffee Room at exactly one minute past two. For a few moments he stared in confusion, and then sheepishly he handed them two voting slips. 'You must write the name of your choice for the Directorship on this piece of paper,' he said, his voice wavering. 'Then put them in this box over here. We shall count the votes at three o'clock.'

'We will wait here until then,' said Dr Schreiber-Ziegler. 'It is always very interesting to be in on the count.'

Prinzel said nothing. It was clear to him that they did not trust him not to interfere with the ballot papers, but of course he could hardly accuse them of that.

'This coffee room is very comfortable,' said Dr Schreiber-Ziegler, pointedly, after they had slipped their voting papers into the box. 'Would you mind if Dr Schneeweiss and I sat down until the count?'

Prinzel could hardly say no, and Herr Huber was quick to encourage them. 'Once Frau Schlaginhauffen and Frau Pommelsbrunn have voted, then we might be able to bring the count forward,' he said to Prinzel. 'There's no point waiting once everybody eligible to vote has done so.'

'None at all,' said Dr Schreiber-Ziegler.

Prinzel pouted. 'The notice gives a clear time of closure,' he said. 'We should stick to that, I think.'

'I don't think so,' said Dr Schneeweiss. 'As external assessor, in fact, I rule otherwise.'

'Then that's decided,' said Dr Schreiber-Ziegler.

Frau Schlaginhauffen and Frau Pommelsbrunn arrived shortly afterwards. Von Igelfeld watched them closely; he saw Dr Schreiber-Ziegler look at the two women and make a sign with her hands. He could not work out what it was, but it was certainly a sign. A threat, he thought; that was what it was – a threat.

With all the voting papers in, Prinzel announced the closing of the poll. 'I now call on Herr Unterholzer to count the votes,' he said.

'No,' said Dr Schneeweiss. 'That is a job for the external assessor.'

Nobody argued, and Dr Schneeweiss stepped forward and extracted the voting papers from the box. Watching her, von Igelfeld thought: this is the end of the Institute as we know it. This is the end. This is a grave, grave moment in the history of Romance philology in the German-speaking world – indeed in the entire academic world. The end.

Dr Schneeweiss tipped the voting papers out on the table Then she picked them up one by one and placed them in the appropriate pile. After that, she announced the results.

'Professor von Igelfeld has seven votes,' she said. 'And Dr Schreiber-Ziegler has one.' She paused. Dr Schreiber-Ziegler was making a strange guttural noise in the back of her throat – a growl perhaps, or a choking sound. 'I therefore declare that Professor Dr Dr (*honoris causa*) (*mult.*) von Igelfeld has been elected Director of the Institute.'

Prinzel and Unterholzer both clapped loudly, and their applause was taken up by Herr Huber.

'A very fine result,' said Prinzel, fixing Dr Schreiber-Ziegler with a steely look. 'And all achieved in an open and transparent way – in accordance with the directives of His Magnificence the Rector.'

Dr Schreiber-Ziegler rose to her feet and left the room. As she did so, she muttered something, which von Igelfeld thought sounded like *Phooey*, but he could not be sure.

Dr Schneeweiss smiled, and then shrugged, as if to distance herself from this storming out, but left too. Now it was only the three professors and Herr Huber in the room, Frau Schlaginhauffen and Frau Pommelsbrunn having left immediately after casting their votes.

'What happened?' asked Unterholzer. 'How did that occur?'

Herr Huber had a theory. 'I suspect that Frau Schlaginhauffen and Frau Pommelsbrunn never really liked Dr Schreiber-Ziegler,' he said. 'I had heard them complaining about her high-handed manner. I think that may have provoked them into rebellion.'

'And Dr Schneeweiss?' asked Unterholzer.

Herr Huber looked at von Igelfeld. 'She is very fond of Professor von Igelfeld,' he said. 'I suspect that this weighed more with her than any arguments advanced by Dr Schreiber-Ziegler.'

'We must give Frau Pommelsbrunn a raise,' said von Igelfeld. 'That, I think, will be one of my first acts as Director. And something for Frau Schlaginhauffen too, if we are able to arrange that with the University administration.'

'An honorary degree in *Müncher Weisswurst*?' suggested Unterholzer.

They all laughed.

'Anything is possible now that you are the Director,' said Prinzel.

'That is very satisfactory,' said von Igelfeld.

'I think we may be entering a new golden age,' said Herr Huber.

The following morning, von Igelfeld was at his desk early. He filled in several order forms for new stationery for the Institute, with his name printed across the top, followed by the words *Director-General*. A little later, just before coffee time, he attended to the morning's mail. There was a letter from the University of Göttingen, and he opened that envelope first, with a confident smile on his face.

The smile faded quickly. 'Dear Professor Dr Dr (*h.c.*) (*mult.*) von Igelfeld,' the letter began. 'Thank you for your recent expression of interest in our new Chair in Romance Linguistics. I regret to inform you that we have not short-listed you. An appointment will shortly be made, the Committee having chosen Dr Andrea Schneeweiss for the position. This is subject to confirmation by the Ministry, but the University will shortly make a formal announcement to this effect.'

Von Igelfeld gasped, but then, on reflection, he thought: why not? Dr Schneeweiss was a very promising scholar and she was an admirer of *Portuguese Irregular Verbs*. It would be good to have a disciple in such a prestigious new position, and it was highly likely that this could lead to another honorary doctorate. Since it seemed that one would not be forthcoming from Oxford, then this was undoubtedly a consolation.

He made his way into the Senior Coffee Room at coffee time. Herr Huber was there by himself.

'Have you heard the good news?' Herr Huber asked.

Von Igelfeld shook his head.

'The police have dropped charges against Professor Dr Unterholzer,' said Herr Huber. 'His name has been cleared.'

'I am very pleased to hear that,' said von Igelfeld. And he was – as Director he could afford to be generous.

'And I take it that you've heard that Dr Schneeweiss has had a call to that Göttingen Chair?'

'Yes, yes, Herr Huber, I know all about that.'

'And is taking Dr Schreiber-Ziegler along with her – to run the Library associated with the Chair?'

'I had not heard that,' said von Igelfeld.

'I must say that I am delighted for Dr Schreiber-Ziegler,' said Herr Huber. 'Her new position will be that of Librarian – not Deputy Librarian – and she richly deserves that.'

'It is good to see talented people going places,' said von Igelfeld, and thought, Yes, preferably as far away as possible. But then he corrected himself: it was wrong to think that; it was uncharitable, and so he said to Herr Huber, 'I am very pleased for Dr Schreiber-Ziegler, and I am sure we shall all miss her.'

He noticed that this last remark made Herr Huber hesitate, and von Igelfeld thought, Herr Huber won't miss her at all. So he smiled, and said, 'To an extent, that is.'

Herr Huber nodded, but did not say anything.

The Sometime Director

Von Igelfeld's first act as Director of the Institute was to contact the University's Works Department and call their Clerk of Works round to discuss several issues relating to the Institute's building. This official, a rather careworn man called Herr Huffnagel, knocked on von Igelfeld's door several minutes before the time of their planned meeting.

'I am a bit early, Herr Director,' the official said as he entered von Igelfeld's room. 'I hope I'm not disturbing anything important.' He looked about the room, noting the piles of books and the profusion of papers. He had always found professors and their surroundings to be completely predictable: papers and books, books and papers. And he had marvelled at the thought that they believed this to be important – to be the real world. How strange was humanity; how deluded.

Von Igelfeld gestured for his visitor to sit. 'Do not perturb yourself, Herr Clerk of Works,' he said. 'We are busy men, both of us, I know. You have your ... your ...' He waved a hand airily. 'Your doors and windows to look after, and I have Romance philology. Each of us has his own *Fach*.'

Herr Huffnagel looked slightly offended. 'My job entails much more than doors and windows, Herr von Igelfeld,' he said. The term of address was deliberately chosen: he saw no reason to address professors as *Herr Professor*; amongst themselves they used their surnames, and if they could do that then why should he not do the same? He was, after all, not just any clerk of works, he was *the* Clerk of Works. 'The University is a major owner of property, I can assure you, and it all needs to be looked after.'

'I'm sure it does,' said von Igelfeld. 'And I'm sure you do that most competently, Herr Huffnagel.'

Mollified, the Clerk of Works asked whether all was in order with the Institute building. 'It all looks in good repair,' he said. 'I notice from our files that you had a bit of trouble with a section of flat roof a couple of years ago, but I take it that that is giving no further trouble.'

'Our roof is very satisfactory,' von Igelfeld assured him. 'I called this meeting, though, not to discuss faults, but to talk about some improvements I would like done. I believe that you are the person in charge of improvements.'

Herr Huffnagel smiled. 'You could say that. But there are others, you know. There's Frau Kasebier, who is the

University Architect-in-Chief, and there's Herr Posner from the Safety Department, and several other colleagues too. We all play a role.'

'But you are the Clerk of Works?' said von Igelfeld. 'You are the man who tells the workmen what to do?'

'Well . . .'

Von Igelfeld did not let him finish. 'So, I have drawn up a short list of things I would like your men to do. I would like, if at all possible, to have the work done the week after next, while I am away at a conference in Geneva.'

Herr Huffnagel stared at him silently. 'It depends—' he began.

'They are not major works,' von Igelfeld interrupted him. 'Most of them are connected with this office, in fact.'

Herr Huffnagel glanced around the room. 'It seems in good—'

'The most important thing,' von Igelfeld continued, 'is a new window. I would like to have it in that wall over there. Your men could move some of those shelves to the side, and put the window in the middle.'

Herr Huffnagel's jaw dropped. 'A window . . .'

'I have done a drawing,' said von Igelfeld. 'It has rough measurements, but your architect, this Frau Kasebier you speak of, can come along with her tape measure and make a more detailed plan.'

He slipped a piece of paper across his desk. Herr Huffnagel looked at it incredulously.

Noticing his hesitation, von Igelfeld enquired if there was anything wrong.

'You may be wondering whether I need a new window, Herr Huffnagel. The truth of the matter is that I have a very limited view from this office. In my previous office I had a much better view, and I freely admit that I should have thought of that aspect of things before I agreed to exchange rooms with Professor Dr Unterholzer. He was in this office before me, you see.' Von Igelfeld felt a certain irritation at the thought. The whole thing had been a trick by Unterholzer, who had assumed that he would leap at the chance of a room with a larger floor area. That had happened exactly as Unterholzer, in his scheming, had imagined it would. Von Igelfeld had not thought of any other aspect of the room's amenity and now he had discovered that not only was the new room deprived of a view, but it was also next door to the men's toilets. This meant that von Igelfeld was regularly disturbed by the sound of doors being opened and closed and taps being run.

'In fact,' said von Igelfeld, 'the question of this room's general amenity leads me to the second point on my list, which is the moving of the men's toilets.' Fixing Herr Huffnagel with an accusing stare, he continued, 'These are currently next door to this room. Right next door.'

Herr Huffnagel had not yet recovered, and was gazing at von Igelfeld with a look of complete disbelief.

'I have found a new location for the men's toilets,' said von Igelfeld. 'There is a vacant store-room at the end of the corridor. A few alterations here and there, and it would make a perfectly satisfactory washroom.' He paused, allowing himself the trace of a smile; there was always room for humour, he felt, even in a serious discussion of this nature. 'I take it you have a good plumber, Herr Huffnagel.'

Herr Huffnagel now recovered his composure. Shaking his head, he politely informed von Igelfeld of the procedures for requesting any work on a university building. 'There is a committee, Herr von Igelfeld. This committee receives applications for projects every three months. It then costs them, obtains a report from the University's Architect if any structural work is involved, and it then puts them on a list for future attention.' He drew in his breath; von Igelfeld's eyes had glazed over, and Herr Huffnagel was not sure that he was taking in what he was saying. 'A committee, you understand, Herr von Igelfeld. A committee. And the waiting list currently stands at sixteen months.' He paused. 'That is from the date when the application is first received in my office, to the date on which work *commences* – not *finishes*, Herr von Igelfeld.'

Von Igelfeld snorted. 'Sixteen months! That is quite unconscionable, Herr Huffnagel.'

Herr Huffnagel continued to be polite, but inwardly he seethed. He would take the greatest possible pleasure in rejecting any application that von Igelfeld made, even if he used the proper channels. Sixteen months? His application would take sixteen *years*, if he had anything to do with it.

'That is how it is, Professor von Igelfeld. And that assumes that the work is considered essential. I do not think that what you are proposing would satisfy that test.' Nor any other test, thought Herr Huffnagel. And then he thought: what a ridiculous name. Von Igelfeld? Hedgehog-field? Where on earth did these people come from? Herr Hedgehog sitting in this office, surrounded by all these pointless papers, believing that the Works Department could drop everything and install a window in a matter of days: did he have the slightest idea of how complex a business inserting a window could be? He could barely wait until he told his friends at the beer cellar about this. How they would laugh.

Von Igelfeld pursed his lips. 'But I am the Director of the Institute,' he protested.

Herr Huffnagel shrugged. 'That makes no difference, I'm afraid. Even the Rector would have to go through the proper channels.'

Von Igelfeld tried another tack. 'This affects my being able to carry out the duties of my office. I cannot be expected to direct the Institute from an office where there is constant disturbance from nearby plumbing.'

Herr Huffnagel shrugged again. 'I have not heard

anything myself,' he said. 'The walls are quite thick in this part of the building. And your colleague – what is his name – Professor Unterholzer? I believe he occupied this room before you and he never complained.'

Von Igelfeld could not let that pass. 'Professor Dr Unterholzer has many good points, Herr Huffnagel,' he said, 'but I do not think that aesthetic sensitivity is one of them.'

Herr Huffnagel rose to his feet. 'I'm sorry we cannot help you with these requests,' he said. 'We could possibly arrange for your office to be painted at some point in the next six months – and I'm afraid we only have green paint at present – but apart from that I'm afraid our estates budget is somewhat limited. We have a major problem with the students' gym – there is rot in the roof and the swimming pool leaks. These are important matters.'

'Students,' muttered von Igelfeld under his breath. 'Are they to get priority?'

Herr Huffnagel heard the question. 'Yes, in fact, they are, Professor von Igelfeld. The University must keep its student body happy or there will be riots. That is a fact of life, I'm afraid.'

'And if the professors were to threaten to riot?' von Igelfeld challenged. 'What then, Herr Huffnagel? Would we get priority then? Is that the way things are ordered in contemporary Germany?'

Herr Huffnagel laughed. 'I can't exactly see you rioting.'

He laughed again. 'Your Librarian, Herr Huber – can you see him hurling cobblestones at the police? I don't think so, Professor von Igelfeld.'

Von Igelfeld glared at Herr Huffnagel. How dared a Clerk of Works – a Clerk of Works! – speak lightly about the professoriate of an ancient German university: was this the brave new world of equality that people talked about? If so, then there was little hope for the future of the country; that was at least one thing of which he was quite sure.

'I am sorry you cannot help me,' he said icily, as he saw Herr Huffnagel out of his room.

'I'm sorry, too,' said Herr Huffnagel. 'In an ideal world . . .'

He did not finish the sentence: von Igelfeld had closed the door.

Back behind his desk, von Igelfeld stared up at the ceiling, a growing sense of frustration within him. If he had had a window worth looking out of, he would have stared out of that. As it was, he gazed at the ceiling, which he now realised needed painting, as it was discoloured. Unterholzer occasionally smoked a pipe, and the tobacco smoke had turned the paintwork a light brown. And he had to put up with it: he, the Director of the Institute of Romance Philology and author of *Portuguese Irregular Verbs* – he had to tolerate the consequences of Unterholzer's disgusting habits. It was insupportable.

He realised that he had no chance of a window now, and

even less of a chance of relocating the men's washroom. But then he thought that he could perhaps do something about that. Yes, he would issue an instruction that those toilets were not to be used during office hours. If people needed to visit then, then there was a perfectly good set of toilets on the top floor, and they could make their way up there. Either that, or they could exercise some restraint and not visit the washroom until five in the evening, which was the time that von Igelfeld liked to bring the day's labours to an end. That was not too much to ask, he felt, in view of the disturbance for him which the constant use of the washroom caused.

The unfortunate meeting with Herr Huffnagel happened in the first week of von Igelfeld's directorship. The following week saw challenges of an equally distressing nature, when he received an unannounced visit from Herr Uber-Huber, who brought with him a list of committees on which von Igelfeld, as Director of the Institute, would be obliged to sit *ex officio*.

'I have discussed the matter with His Magnificence the Rector,' Herr Uber-Huber began, seeking in this way to forestall any objection from von Igelfeld. 'He has determined that you should be on twelve university committees, and that you should assume the chairmanship of one of these – the Parking Committee.'

Von Igelfeld picked up the list that Herr Uber-Huber

had unceremoniously placed on his desk. He saw that it was headed by something called the Student Achievement Committee. Directly underneath that was the Sanitary Committee.

'This Achievement Committee,' he said. 'What is its function, Herr Uber-Huber?'

Herr Uber-Huber explained. 'It looks for ways in which we can deal with needs of students who fail their exams. There are many reasons for examination failure, as I'm sure you know.'

Von Igelfeld sucked in his cheeks. 'The most significant being a lack of knowledge,' he said.

Herr Uber-Huber smiled. 'Forgive me for suggesting that that's an old-fashioned view, Herr von Igelfeld. It's not that simple these days. We must be progressive. Some students are nervous.'

Von Igelfeld raised an eyebrow. 'It's quite normal to be nervous about examinations. I would have thought that an examination of which one was not a bit nervous would hardly be a test of anything. You may as well give the students the answers before they sit the examination – that would diminish their nervousness.' He paused. 'Is that progressive enough?'

'Hah!' said Herr Uber-Huber. 'That is a very constructive suggestion, Herr von Igelfeld. You should propose that at the next meeting of the committee.'

Von Igelfeld tapped the sheet of paper. 'And this

committee here,' he said. 'The Sanitary Committee. What is its function?'

'I serve on that committee myself,' said Herr Uber-Huber. 'It is a very interesting committee. It looks at hygiene issues throughout the University. Dishwashing facilities in the kitchens, showers in the student gyms, disposal of rubbish from the labs, and so on.'

Von Igelfeld made a scornful noise. 'And this Parking Committee? I assume it deals with the University's car parks.'

'Precisely,' said Herr Uber-Huber. 'It regulates the permits given to staff. It allocates parking spaces for visitors and emergency services. It is a very important committee – which explains why it meets every Monday for two and a half hours.'

Von Igelfeld drew in his breath. 'I cannot possibly chair that committee,' he said. 'Monday is a very busy day for me. I always devote it to catching up on the philological reviews. There is so much to read these days. You should pass on that information to His Magnificence.'

'The Rector himself appointed you to that,' said Herr Uber-Huber. 'You cannot decline a rectorial appointment.'

Von Igelfeld folded Herr Uber-Huber's list and put it in his pocket. 'I'm afraid I must ask you to leave now, Herr Uber-Huber,' he said. 'I have scholarly matters to attend to – before all my time begins to be taken up with the problems of student ignorance, drains, and illegal parking.'

'A good idea,' said Herr Uber-Huber. '*Carpe dies.*'

Von Igelfeld quivered. '*Diem*, Herr Uber-Huber. Accusative case. *Diem.*'

By the end of the second week, von Igelfeld had come to the realisation that the Directorship of the Institute was a poisoned chalice. There may have been a time when the post of Director would have been largely ceremonial, requiring only an occasional decision on some minor point and giving the incumbent largely untrammelled power over the internal affairs of the Institute; but that was clearly no longer the case. Von Igelfeld had no taste for sitting on committees, and the first meeting of the Parking Committee that Monday confirmed his misgivings. That meeting lasted four hours until, despairing of ever reaching a decision, von Igelfeld used his position as chairman to shut the meeting down. Returning to his office, he found that Frau Pommelsbrunn, the cleaner, was waiting for him and would not be put off with the promise of an appointment the following week.

'I cannot possibly wait until then,' she said. 'I would rather resign.'

Inviting her in, he sat down at his desk and listened as the cleaner poured out her tale of woe. She had discovered, she told him, that Frau Schlaginhauffen, from the University canteen, was paid almost twice the wages she received.

'That is extremely unfair,' Frau Pommelsbrunn said.

'She works more or less the same hours, and look at the difference.'

Von Igelfeld sighed. He remembered that he had said to his colleagues that his first task as Director would be to give Frau Pommelsbrunn a raise, but the problems with his office, and then the unwelcome distraction of all those wretched committees, had driven it far from his mind. And he had, during these first two weeks of his tenure, become aware that his role as Director was not, in fact, consummate; in fact, it was subject to a disappointingly large number of constraints. What was he to say?

'Frau Schlaginhauffen is a very skilled lady,' he said. 'She has a considerable reputation for her *Müncher Weisswurst*. Everybody talks about that.' He paused. 'You, by contrast, are unskilled – or have very lowly skills, Frau Pommelsbrunn.'

'Oag!' shouted Frau Pommelsbrunn. And then, for good measure, 'Oag!' again.

Von Igelfeld frowned. What was this word *oag*? It was clearly not a term of agreement – he could work that out – but it was not a word that he had ever encountered in any dictionary – even a dictionary of the demotic.

Frau Pommelsbrunn wagged a finger at von Igelfeld. 'I voted for you, Herr von Igelfeld. I thought you were a man who would recognise the right thing – and then do it. Was I right to think that? I now ask myself. Was I right?'

Von Igelfeld sank his head in his hands. 'I shall raise it

with the University authorities,' he said. 'With the ... with the ...' An idea occurred: the Sanitary Committee was presumably concerned with cleaning matters, and perhaps he could use his influence there to facilitate the settlement of Frau Pommelsbrunn's claim. 'I have influence on the relevant committee,' he said. 'I shall do my best, Frau Pommelsbrunn.'

He walked home that evening rather than take the bus that ran directly from the University campus past the end of his street. As he walked, he became aware of a man whose course seemed to be following his own, but on the other side of the street. He glanced at the man, who seemed vaguely familiar, although von Igelfeld could not quite place him. As he approached the end of his street, though, the man crossed over and addressed him directly.

'Professor von Igelfeld,' the man said in English. 'Forgive me the intrusion.'

Von Igelfeld stopped in his tracks. Now that he saw the man's face, it was coming back to him. This was Blunt, the shadowy figure he had met in the wine cellars of All Souls; Blunt, the crisply spoken person referred to as B.

'Herr Blunt,' von Igelfeld said.

'Please,' whispered Blunt. 'Please just call me B.'

They were now walking side by side, to the casual observer simply two colleagues making their way home from work.

'I read about your appointment,' said Blunt. 'Excellent

news. This will provide us with even further opportunities for making contacts, if you see what I mean. We like our sleepers to be in prominent positions.'

'Sleeper?' asked von Igelfeld. 'What is a sleeper?'

Blunt laughed. 'Oh, my dear chap, don't tell me you don't know? Of course you do.'

'I do not, said von Igelfeld.

'That's the spirit, V,' said Blunt. 'Deny, point blank. It's the only way. Just like our late friend Philby. What a liar that man was! World-class!'

'I'm not sure I know what you mean,' said von Igelfeld.

'Be that as it may,' said Blunt. 'The point is this: in six months there is to be a conference in St Petersburg. A number of prominent Russian linguists will be taking part. One of them is of considerable interest to us – he is also a significant cryptographer – and we would like to discuss certain possibilities with him. What better way to do that than through one of the participants in the conference? Which is where you come in.'

Von Igelfeld shook his head. 'I am not planning to go to St Petersburg,' he said.

Blunt did not appear to take in this information. 'We'll get you all the necessary paperwork in a month or two,' he said.

Von Igelfeld was silent. He had no idea what this enigmatic man was talking about, and if he received an invitation to St Petersburg he would simply ignore it. And yet he did appear to have something to do with Oxford, and von

Igelfeld would not want to antagonise an institution that was proposing to give him an honorary degree.

He decided to enquire after Plowson.

When he heard the question, Blunt frowned. 'Plowson? Oh, my dear fellow ... poor Plowson's gone off to Tuvalu. He was appointed to a University Chair down there.' He lowered his voice. 'Apparently, he got the job by promising somebody an honorary degree. He was in no position to fulfil the promise, of course, but by then the University had carried out its part of the bargain and had made him a professor. It was too late for them to do anything about it. He's said to be extremely happy in his new post. He's met a woman who owns a fishing boat and he's skippering that for her, when he's not being a professor. He doesn't know the first thing about the sea, but there we are.'

Von Igelfeld listened without giving anything away. The prospect of an honorary degree from Oxford was now remote, if not non-existent. But there would be other opportunities, no doubt. Next week a prominent professor from Ahmadu Bello University in Nigeria was to visit the Institute and von Igelfeld had looked up their doctoral robes, which were very satisfactory, involving copious panels of green silk. A hint might be dropped – subtly, of course – and something might be forthcoming.

They had almost reached von Igelfeld's front door. Blunt indicated that he must leave, reassuring von Igelfeld that he would soon be in touch about the St Petersburg assignment.

'But until then, you and I had better not be seen together too prominently. So *auf Wiedersehen*, dear V. *Tschüss, et cetera, et cetera!*'

And with that, Blunt was gone.

Von Igelfeld made his plans carefully. He had studied the memorandum on the governance of the Institute, drawn up by the Rector, and had noted the procedures to be adopted in the event of the resignation of a Director *or a Director's temporary absence.* If this were to occur, then the Director demitting office or taking a leave of absence could nominate a person to act on his or her behalf for such term as was necessary to permit the continued smooth running of the Institute. The choice of the nominee was entirely personal, as far as von Igelfeld could make out, the provision clearly having been drafted to deal with short-term, transitional arrangements. His term of office, however, had three years to run. Furthermore, during that period, the absent or outgoing Director was entitled to relieve the temporary appointee of office if so desired.

This was perfect, and, after he had read over the relevant provisions several times, von Igelfeld went to discuss the matter with the Librarian.

'I have a proposal for you, Herr Huber,' he began. 'It is not one that I make lightly, but I have always known of your devotion to the interests of the Institute.'

Herr Huber looked at von Igelfeld with grateful eyes.

That was all he had ever wanted: to serve the Institute and, in particular, its Library. That was his life.

'I am always willing to do what may be required,' said Herr Huber.

Von Igelfeld nodded. 'I know that, Herr Huber. And that is why I would like you to assume the position of Director with immediate effect.'

Herr Huber gasped, and for a few moments von Igelfeld thought that he might faint. But he recovered and said, 'Me, Professor von Igelfeld? Me?'

'Yes, you, Herr Huber. I know that you are only a librarian, but I believe you have very fine qualities. You will serve for the remainder of my term subject to ...' This was the important part, and he spelled it out as clearly as he could. 'Subject to your consulting me on major issues and voting as I suggest on any crucial matters.'

'But of course,' said Herr Huber. 'I would never wish to do otherwise.'

'Good,' said von Igelfeld. 'And there is another, minor matter. That is the question of rooms. I would like one of your first acts as Director to be the transfer of Professor Dr Unterholzer from his existing room back to the room that he previously occupied. As Director, you will have that power. Professor Unterholzer might object, but you must remain firm and overrule his objections. Then I shall return to the room that he is currently occupying.'

'I shall be happy to do that,' said Herr Huber.

'And I thought of another thing,' von Igelfeld continued. 'I think it would be appropriate to have a small lapel badge made for the Director of the Institute – like one of those French orders – a *bouton*, perhaps. Nothing too fancy – just something that could be worn on appropriate occasions. What do you think of that?'

'It is a very good idea,' said Herr Huber. He looked at von Igelfeld with something close to adoration. 'You are so kind, Professor von Igelfeld,' he said. 'I don't know how to thank you.'

Von Igelfeld made a self-deprecating gesture. 'No need,' he said.

He thought: I am a fortunate man, and if you are fortunate in this life, you should take pleasure in the good fortune of others. Because we must love one another – for all our faults. We must love one another whatever our station in life, and we must try to make the lives of others more bearable, if we are in a position to do so.

He looked at Herr Huber. 'And for my part I am most grateful to you, Herr Huber – I really am.'

Herr Huber did not know what to say. He could not remember when it was that anybody had last thanked him. He cleared his throat, but before he could say anything von Igelfeld had continued, 'And tell me, Herr Huber, is there anything of note to report from your aunt's nursing home?'

'Well, as it happens, Herr von Igelfeld . . .'

Von Igelfeld looked out of the window. The sky over

Germany was clear. There were no clouds – only an aircraft vapour trail going somewhere, impossibly high, up where the air was cold and pure. Von Igelfeld closed his eyes. Herr Huber was saying something, but he was not sure what it was. We must love those whose lives touch our own, thought von Igelfeld; we must love them whoever they are. I have not done that enough in the past, perhaps, but there is always the future; whether we have minutes left us, or long years – there is always enough time.

Don't let the story stop here

Visit www.alexandermccallsmith.co.uk

Discover new stories

Find out about events

Sign up to Alexander's newsletter

/alexandermccallsmith @mccallsmith

Help us make the next generation of readers

We – both author and publisher – hope you enjoyed this book. We believe that you can become a reader at any time in your life, but we'd love your help to give the next generation a head start.

Did you know that 9% of children don't have a book of their own in their home, rising to 12% in disadvantaged families*? We'd like to try to change that by asking you to consider the role you could play in helping to build readers of the future.

We'd love you to think of sharing, borrowing, reading, buying or talking about a book with a child in your life and spreading the love of reading. We want to make sure the next generation continue to have access to books, wherever they come from.

And if you would like to consider donating to charities that help fund literacy projects, find out more at www.literacytrust.org.uk and www.booktrust.org.uk.

Thank you.

little, brown
BOOK GROUP

*As reported by the National Literacy Trust